Heartland

Taking Chances

Heartland

❧

Share every moment . . .

Coming Home

After the Storm

Breaking Free

Taking Chances

Heartland

Taking Chances

by Lauren Brooke

SCHOLASTIC INC.

New York   Toronto   London   Auckland   Sydney
Mexico City   New Delhi   Hong Kong   Buenos Aires

With special thanks to Linda Chapman

Library of Congress Cataloging-in-Publication data available.

ISBN 0-439-13025-5

Heartland series created by Working Partners Ltd., London.

Copyright © 2001 by Working Partners Ltd.
Published by Scholastic Inc. All rights reserved.

SCHOLASTIC and associated logos are trademarks and/or registered trademarks of Scholastic Inc. HEARTLAND is a trademark and/or registered trademark of Working Partners Ltd.

24 23 22 21 20 19 18 17 16 15 14   6/0

Printed in the U.S.A.
First Scholastic printing, February 2001   40

To my parents,
for buying me my first pony
and making my dreams come true

Heartland

❧

Taking Chances

Chapter One

Amy finished filling up a water bucket and glanced at her watch. It was twelve-thirty. Soraya would be arriving any minute. She placed the bucket in Solo's stall and headed to the top of the drive to wait for her friend.

On either side of the driveway, horses and ponies grazed contentedly in the turnout paddocks, the October breeze ruffling their coats and sending the occasional red or gold leaf skittering across the short grass.

Only one paddock was empty. In the middle stood a single oak sapling, the soil still fresh around its base.

Amy walked over to the wooden gate and leaned against it. "Pegasus," she whispered, a wave of sadness flooding over her as she looked at the young tree. She could hardly believe it was only three weeks since her favorite horse had been buried there.

Amy pictured the great gray horse. In his younger days, he had been one of the most famous show jumpers in the world. But Amy remembered him better as the horse that had let her play around his legs when she was little and had nuzzled her when she was upset. To her, he was the horse that had helped her through the nightmare of her mom being killed in a road accident four months ago and the horse that had been her dearest friend.

Amy swallowed as she looked at the sapling. *Everything's changed so much in the last few months,* she thought to herself. *Mom's gone. Pegasus is gone. Lou's come back.*

The return of Lou to Heartland was one of the few good things that had happened. Until recently, Amy's older sister had worked in Manhattan, but when their mother died she decided to leave her banking job and live permanently at Heartland, the equine sanctuary their mom, Marion, had set up on their grandpa's farm.

The sound of a car coming up the drive roused Amy from her thoughts. She looked around.

Soraya Martin, her best friend, was waving from the front passenger seat as her mom's car neared. Amy took a deep breath, swallowing hard and pushing down the ache of painful memories. She waved back, forcing herself to smile, burying her inner sadness.

"Hi!" Soraya called, winding down the window. "Sorry I'm late. Mom had to pick up some groceries on the way over." The car drew to a halt, and Soraya jumped out, black curls bouncing on her shoulders. "See you later, Mom," she said. "Thanks for the ride."

"Sure," Mrs. Martin said, smiling at Amy. "Now, you girls have fun."

Amy and Soraya grinned at each other. "We will," they both said at once.

❧

Half an hour later, Amy tightened her fingers on Sundance's reins and looked toward the fallen tree that lay across one side of the trail. "Come on, boy," she whispered. "Let's jump it!"

"Be careful, Amy," Soraya called. "It's a big one."

"Not for Sundance," Amy replied, turning her buckskin pony toward the tree trunk.

Seeing the jump, Sundance threw his head up in excitement and plunged forward, but Amy was ready for him. Her body moved effortlessly in the saddle. "Easy now," she murmured, her fingers caressing his warm neck.

The pony's golden ears flickered as he listened to her voice — and then he relaxed, his neck lowering and his mouth softening on the bit.

Amy squeezed with her legs. In five strides they reached the tree trunk. It loomed up in front of them — massive, solid. Amy felt Sundance's muscles gather as he

4   HEARTLAND

took off perfectly and gracefully rose into the air. Amy caught a glimpse of thick, gnarled bark flashing by beneath them, felt a moment of suspension as if she and Sundance were flying, and then heard the sweet thud of his hooves as he landed cleanly on the other side. They were over!

"Good boy!" Amy cried in delight.

"He looks so good!" Soraya said, letting Jasmine trot forward to meet them. "He's jumping better than ever, Amy."

"I know!" Amy grinned, patting Sundance's neck. "He's incredible!"

As the two ponies reached each other, Jasmine stretched out her neck to say hello. With an angry squeal, Sundance threw his head in the air, his ears back. "Stop it, Sundance!" Amy exclaimed, turning him away. "Jasmine's your friend."

The buckskin nuzzled her leg affectionately. Even though he was stubborn and difficult with most horses and people, he adored Amy. She had first seen him at a horse sale. Thin and unhappy, he lashed out at anyone who tried to come through the gate of his pen. But Amy had a special feeling about him and persuaded her mom to buy him. They took him back to Heartland, where Amy gradually gained his trust and affection.

"Are you planning to go to any shows with him?" Soraya asked as they started along the trail again.

Amy shook her head. "There's no time. All the stalls have been full since the day of the open house, and there's a waiting list of people who want to bring their horses here."

Just two weeks ago, Lou had organized an open house at Heartland. People had been invited to come find out about Heartland's methods for curing physically and emotionally damaged horses. Amy and Ty, Heartland's seventeen-year-old stable hand, had given demonstrations, and the day had been a great success. Ever since then, they had been inundated with inquiries from owners of problem horses.

"It's good, though, that you've got lots of horses boarding," Soraya said. "I mean, it must be such a relief to know that you can carry on your mom's work and not stress too much about money."

Amy nodded, remembering the difficulties Heartland had faced before the open house. After her mom died, Heartland had come close to shutting down because of the lack of customers. They had been extremely close to running out of money and losing everything. But now, thankfully, it was different. Business was booming.

"Yeah, I'm glad we're busy," she said. "Even if it does mean that I don't have much time to go to shows." She patted Sundance's neck. "Still, things might get easier now that Ben will be working for us."

Ben was eighteen and the nephew of Lisa Stillman,

the wealthy and successful owner of Fairfield Arabian Stud. After Amy had cured one of Fairfield's prestigious show horses, Lisa had been so impressed that she arranged for Ben to come to work at Heartland so he could learn their methods. He was expected to arrive that afternoon.

Soraya glanced at Amy. "Do you think he has a girl-friend?"

"Why?" Amy grinned. "Are you interested?" She and Soraya had both met Ben briefly when he had dropped off the problem horse that Amy treated. Tall and good-looking, he had seemed OK, but he wasn't really Amy's type.

"You have to admit he *is* cute," Soraya said. She raised her eyebrows. "Poor guy. I guess he's not going to know anyone around here. I'll just *have* to offer to give him a tour."

Amy feigned innocence. "Don't go out of your way, Soraya. I'm sure Ty can do it — he's looking forward to having another guy around the place."

"Oh, *no*," Soraya said quickly. "I'm sure I'd make a *much* better guide than Ty."

"Well, I'm looking forward to seeing Ben's horse," Amy said. "He's a show jumper. Ben said he'd only work at Heartland if he could bring his horse, too."

"So what time's he coming?" Soraya asked.

"Two o'clock."

Soraya glanced at her watch. "We should get a move on, then. It's almost one-thirty."

Amy gathered up her reins. "What are you waiting for? Let's go!"

❦

Amy and Soraya rode down the trail that led to the back of Heartland. Coming out of the trees, they could see Heartland's barns and sheds spread out before them — the turnout paddocks with their dark wooden fencing, the two training rings, the twelve-stall back barn, and the front stable block that made an L-shape toward the white, weather-boarded farmhouse.

As Amy halted Sundance, she heard the sound of hooves thudding angrily against the wall of the barn.

"Steady now!" Amy could hear Ty's raised voice from inside the barn. "Easy, girl!"

"It sounds like Ty could use some help," she said.

"You go," Soraya said. "I'll take care of Sundance."

"Thanks." Amy threw Sundance's reins at her friend and headed into the barn. A wide aisle separated the six stalls on each side. From a stall near the back came the crash of hooves striking the wall. Amy realized it was Dancer's stall.

Dancer was a paint mare who had been neglected.

She was half starved and left on a tiny patch of land where an animal charity had found her. The charity volunteers called Heartland, and Amy and Ty had immediately agreed to help. Dancer had arrived only two days ago, and her recovery was progressing slowly.

"You OK, Ty?" Amy called.

Ty looked over Dancer's door. His dark hair was disheveled. "Yeah," he replied, wiping his bare forearm across his face.

"What's up?" Amy asked, looking into the stall. Dancer was standing by the back wall, her body trembling.

"All I did was pick up her hoof, and she went crazy," Ty said, shaking his head. "She broke her lead rope and started kicking in every direction. She had me cornered for a bit, but I managed to get out. Now she's all worked up."

Amy looked at the frightened mare. "Maybe we should try some chestnut powder to calm her down," she suggested, remembering it had been one of her mom's favorite remedies for traumatized horses.

Ty nodded. "Good idea. You wait with her, I'll get it."
He hurried off.

The mare shifted uneasily at the back of the stall. Her muscles were tense and her ribs protruded painfully through her shaggy coat. Around her face were scars where her old halter had been digging into her skin, and her fetlocks were covered with rope burns from hobbles that had been tightly tied around her legs to stop her from wandering away.

"It's OK, girl," Amy said softly. "You're safe now. No one's going to hurt you anymore."

Amy watched as the mare's ears flickered uncertainly. She knew her recovery would take time.

Ty returned with a small tin. He handed it to Amy. "Here," he said. "It might be better if you try. I don't want to upset her again."

Amy unscrewed the lid of the tin. Inside there was a gritty gray powder. Taking a little, she rubbed it onto the palms of her hands. Then she stepped forward, her shoulders turned sideways to the mare, her eyes lowered.

Dancer shifted nervously. Amy stopped, offered her palm for the mare to sniff, and waited.

After a few moments, the mare turned and snorted. Stretching her muzzle out toward Amy's upturned hand, she breathed in, her nostrils dilating. Amy waited a few moments, and then, talking softly, she gently reached out and touched Dancer's neck with her other hand. As her fingers stroked and caressed, she felt the mare gradually begin to relax. Amy's fingers massaged the mare's neck until she came to her head. When Dancer seemed to trust her, Amy took hold of the lead rope.

"Nice job," Ty said in a low voice. Rubbing a little of

the powder onto his own palms, he approached the mare. She looked at him cautiously but then stretched out her head and let him stroke her, too. "Poor girl," he said, rubbing her neck. "Your life hasn't been too great up to now, has it?"

"Well, it's going to be a lot better from here on," Amy said.

For a moment they stood in silence, both stroking the mare.

She looked at the deep scars on Dancer's brown-and-white legs. "Maybe when you touched her feet she thought that you were going to put hobbles on her," she suggested.

Ty nodded. "I guess we'll just have to take things slowly."

"As always," Amy said, smiling at him.

She didn't know what she'd do without Ty. He was so good with the horses. After her mom had died, he had taken over the running of the yard while the family came to terms with their loss. She knew they were lucky to have him. He never seemed to treat working at Heartland as just a regular job — he seemed as devoted to Heartland as Amy.

Ty looked at the tin in his hand. "Your mom's magic powder did it again."

Amy nodded. Her mom had been told about the powder by an old horseman in Tennessee. It contained herbs ground up with chestnut trimmings — the masses that grow on the insides of horses' legs. Marion had written down the recipe, and they had used it at Heartland ever since.

"Your mom was amazing," Ty said, turning the tin over in his hands. "She had great instincts and knew so much about horses. Sometimes I wonder if I'll ever be half as good as she was."

"You're pretty good already, Ty," Amy said, surprised.

"But not good enough," Ty said. He shook his head. "I was learning so much from her, Amy. Since she's been gone, I'm just struggling to keep up. I feel like there's a lot left to learn, but I don't know how. And I hate it."

"You can't think like that, Ty," Amy said quickly.

"Why not?" Ty replied. "I keep thinking if I only knew more, I'd have a better shot at really helping these horses."

Amy stepped closer to Ty, wanting to let him know that she understood. "You know, I felt the same when Pegasus was really sick, and I couldn't help him. But then I realized I just had to accept that there are things I don't know, and all I can do is try my best." She paused, her eyes searching his. "You have to trust yourself. You know Mom would have said the same thing."

Ty nodded slowly. "Yeah, I guess."

They stood for a moment, neither of them speaking. The silence was interrupted by the sound of footsteps running down the aisle. "Hey, you guys! There's a trailer coming up the drive!" Soraya reached Dancer's door and looked over. "It's looks really nice. Come check it out."

"It must be Ben," Amy said, looking at Ty.

He nodded. Leaving Dancer, they hurried down the yard. A gleaming white trailer, with green and purple stripes and a black crest with the words FAIRFIELD ARABIANS emblazoned on the side, was pulling up in front of the house. The truck stopped, and Ben Stillman jumped out.

"Hey," he said, straightening his tall frame.

Amy stepped forward. "Hi, I'm Amy. We met when you brought Promise over for your aunt. This is my friend Soraya Martin," she said, pushing Soraya forward.

"Hi," Soraya grinned.

"Yeah, I remember," Ben smiled. "Hi."

"And you've met Ty," Amy said.

"Welcome back to Heartland." Ty offered his hand. As they shook hands, the farmhouse door opened and Lou came out. She had also met Ben when he dropped Promise off at Heartland. "Hello again," she said, smiling at Ben.

"Good to meet you properly this time," Ben said.

"I'll see you later — I'm just going into town," Lou said, walking toward her car with her keys in hand.

Just then, from inside the trailer, came the sound of a horse stamping impatiently.

"Sounds like Red wants to get out," Ben said. "He's fine when we're on the road but can't stand being in the trailer after we've stopped."

"Here, I'll give you a hand," Ty volunteered.

Ben disappeared inside the trailer while Ty unbolted the ramp. Amy watched eagerly, wondering what Ben's horse would be like.

Ty lowered the ramp to the ground. There was a clatter of hooves, and, suddenly, a bright chestnut horse shot nervously down the ramp, with Ben holding tightly on to the end of the lead rope. Once out, the horse stopped and looked around, his head held high.

"Wow!" Amy exclaimed. "He's gorgeous!"

"He's called Red, but his show name is *What Luck*," Ben said, looking pleased. "He's a Thoroughbred–Hanoverian cross."

Amy walked closer, admiring Red's handsome head, broad back, and strong, clean legs. Standing, she guessed, at around sixteen-two hands, he looked every inch a show jumper. "How old is he?" she asked, letting Red sniff her hand and then patting his muscular neck.

"Six," Ben said. "My aunt bought him for me when he was three." He glanced at the trailer. "I guess there are *some* advantages to having a rich aunt who's into horses."

Hearing a strange note in his voice, Amy glanced at

him. For a moment she saw what she thought was a look of bitterness cross his face.

"*Some* advantages?" Ty said. He was putting the ramp up and obviously hadn't seen Ben's expression. "That's the understatement of the year!"

"Yeah." Ben coughed, his face suddenly clearing and his voice becoming light again. "I guess you're right. So which stall should I put him in?" he asked Amy.

"The one at the end," Amy replied, pointing toward the stable block. "It's all bedded down and ready for him."

"Come on, boy." Ben clicked his tongue and Red moved forward.

Leaving Soraya and Ty to clear out the trailer, Amy went on ahead of Ben and opened the stall door. "Do you compete much on Red?" she asked.

Ben nodded as he started taking off the pillow wraps that had protected the gelding's legs on the journey over. "He's got real talent. I've been taking him in Prelim Jumper classes, but with the way he's been winning I figure he's going to upgrade real quick." He stood up with the wraps in his arms. "We're going to make it to the top," he said confidently. "I'm sure of it."

Amy looked at him in surprise; he didn't sound like he had any doubts.

"So," Ben said, walking out of the stall, "what's it like living around here?"

"It's OK," Amy replied.

"You'll have to show me around," Ben said.

Amy remembered what Soraya had said and saw the perfect opportunity. "Well, I'm always pretty busy with the horses," she said as they walked across the yard toward where Soraya and Ty were standing by the trailer. "But Soraya has tons of spare time."

"Did I hear my name?" Soraya asked, turning to face them.

"Yeah, I was just telling Ben that you'd be happy to give him a tour," Amy answered, giving her a meaningful look.

"Yeah, of course!" Soraya said, stepping forward eagerly. "Anytime."

"Thanks." Ben smiled at her. "I might just take you up on that."

"Do you want to check out the other stable?" Amy offered. "You've got all the horses to meet, and then we can start telling you about our work here at Heartland."

"Actually, you know, I might leave all that till tomorrow," Ben said, yawning. "I want to go to my new place and start unpacking. Then I think I'll just crash for a while."

"Oh . . . right," Amy said, a bit taken aback. She knew that if she was about to start work at a new stable, the first thing she would want to do was look at the horses. "Well, sure. Go ahead."

"Great," Ben said. "Well, I'll just unload Red's tack, then I'll be off."

Amy, Ty, and Soraya helped him carry the mountain of blankets, tack, and grooming equipment up to the tack room. When they were done, Ben unhitched the trailer and got into his truck. "I'll be back to feed Red later," he said, starting the engine.

Not long after he had driven off, Lou got back. "I think I passed Ben on the road. Did he leave already?" she asked, getting out of her car.

Amy nodded.

"But I was going to ask him if he wanted to stay for supper tonight," Lou said, frowning. "Oh, well, I guess I can call him. I've got his phone number." She looked at Soraya and Ty. "You're both welcome to stay, too."

"That would be great," Ty said. "Thanks."

"Oh, I can't," Soraya said ruefully. "I'm going out tonight for my mom's birthday. But thanks anyway, Lou."

Lou looked down the drive. "It's a bit odd that Ben didn't stick around longer. I thought he'd be here for a couple of hours, anyway. Grandpa will be sorry to have missed him." Shaking her head, she went back into the house.

"So what do you think?" Amy asked Ty and Soraya as they walked back across the yard.

"Of Ben?" Soraya inquired. "Definitely cute!"

"And after all, what else matters?" Ty teased.

Soraya pretended to punch him.

Amy grinned. "Come on, what do you think, Ty?"

"He seems fine," Ty said, shrugging.

"And?" Amy pushed for more.

"And nothing," Ty said. He looked at Amy and Soraya's expectant faces. "Well, what else do you expect me to say?" he demanded. "I only met the guy for about five minutes."

"Well, I only met him for five minutes, too, and I think he seems really nice," Amy said. She turned to Soraya. "He was telling me about Red. He's been competing in Prelim Jumpers. Ben thinks they'll move up pretty quick."

"I wonder when we'll get to see him ride," Soraya said. Her eyes looked dreamy. "I bet he looks great on Red!"

"Oh, please!" Ty grimaced. "You think he looks great, period." Shaking his head, he went into the tack room.

Exchanging grins, Amy and Soraya followed him. In the middle of the tack room floor was a mound of Ben's stuff.

"Three saddles," Ty commented, starting to make space on the already crowded saddle racks.

"And all top quality," Amy added, picking up a forward-cut jumping saddle and admiring the well-oiled leather.

"I wish I had a rich aunt who would buy me a horse like Red and all this stuff," Soraya said.

Ty nodded as he hung up a bridle. "Ben sure is a lucky guy."

Amy thought about the look she had seen pass across Ben's face just after he'd unloaded Red. At that moment he hadn't seemed exactly thrilled with his good fortune. Still, it must have been wonderful to have grown up on a huge horse farm with lots of money. Maybe he was having a hard time leaving Fairfield and wasn't sure about the arrangement his aunt had made with Heartland. "Imagine living at a place like Fairfield," she said out loud.

"Yeah," Ty said nodding. "I wish."

Amy looked at him. Ty's family had very little money. He had first started working as a part-time stable hand at Heartland when he was only fifteen, to help out his parents. But money was still tight, so he approached Marion a year later about hiring him full-time.

"Do you know why Ben grew up with his aunt instead of his parents?" Soraya asked.

"I think it was something to do with his parents getting divorced when he was younger," Amy said, remembering a conversation between Lou and Lisa Stillman when they'd first discussed the possibility of Ben coming to Heartland. "But I don't really know that much about it. We might find out more tonight."

"I wish I could stay," Soraya said longingly. "Promise you'll find out all the gossip about him — like whether he's got a girlfriend or not."

"Oh, you mean the real *important* stuff." Amy grinned at her. "Don't worry. Of course I will."

Chapter Two

Ben arrived back at Heartland just as Amy and Ty were mixing the evening feeds. "Are you unpacked?" Ty asked when Ben joined them in the feed room.

Ben nodded. "Yeah, thanks." He looked around at the huge metal bins, stone-flagged floor, and thick strands of dusty cobwebs hanging from the wooden ceiling beams. "So this is where you keep the grain, right?"

"Yeah," Amy said. "Just help yourself to whatever you want for Red. There's cod liver oil and other supplements in the cabinets over there." She pointed to a corner of the feed room. "And you can use any of those buckets in that pile — they're all spare."

"Here," Ty said, getting a bucket for him.

"Thanks," Ben said. "But I've brought Red's buckets for him. They're in the trailer."

20

He returned a few minutes later with a couple of steel buckets, each embossed with the Fairfield crest and with Red's name in neat black lettering on the side. Ben scooped some oats and alfalfa cubes into one of the buckets and then looked in the cupboard.

"Wow!" he exclaimed, staring at the packed shelves, crammed with dried herbs and country remedies — honey, bicarbonate of soda, vinegar, chalk. "You sure use a lot of supplements here."

"Well, we don't just use herbs as feed supplements," Amy said. "We use them to help deal with behavioral and physical problems. If you want, when we're done feeding, Ty and I can start giving you an idea of what some of the herbs do."

"Sure," Ty said enthusiastically. "The healing properties are pretty amazing."

"Yeah, maybe some other time," Ben said casually. "I think I'll go see Red now." Quickly adding a little more grain to the bucket, he carried it out of the feed room.

Amy frowned at Ty. "That's strange. I thought he'd be really interested. After all, he is here to learn about what we do." Past the feed room door, she could hear the horses in the front stable block banging their doors impatiently. They would have seen Ben walk past with Red's bucket. "And he could have offered to help us feed the other horses," she said, feeling slightly irritated. "Now the others are going to be wild until they get fed."

"I know what you mean," Ty shrugged. "But he just got here and probably wants to make sure Red's settling in."

"I guess," Amy said. She picked up a pile of buckets. "Well, we'd better get feeding before they kick all the stalls down."

❧

At seven o'clock, Lou came out from the house. "Dinner's almost ready!" she called.

Amy and Ty came out of the tack room just as Ben appeared from Red's stall.

"How is he?" Ty asked.

"He's doing just fine," Ben replied, walking down the yard with them.

The delicious smell of baked ham filled the kitchen. Jack Bartlett, Amy and Lou's grandfather, was draining a pan of black-eyed peas at the sink. "Hi," he said to Ben, turning and offering his hand. "Jack Bartlett."

"Pleased to meet you, sir," Ben said, shaking hands.

As Ty and Amy began to set the table and Lou fixed drinks, Ben spent a few moments looking at the photographs that covered the kitchen walls.

"Is this your mom in these pictures?" he asked Amy.

She nodded and joined him by the pine cabinet. "Yeah. She was competing in England. We lived there when I was little."

"So why did you move back here?" Ben said.

"Because of Daddy's accident," Amy said.

"Oh, my aunt told me about that," Ben said. "He was riding in a jump-off, wasn't he?"

Amy nodded. Her father had been riding Pegasus in the World Championships. Pegasus had caught his legs on the top rail of a fence and fallen. Both he and her father had been badly injured. Having been only three at the time, Amy had no real memory of the event. But as Ben spoke, she saw Lou look around and frown. Lou had been eleven, and Amy knew she remembered it all much more clearly.

"So what happened to your dad after the accident?" Ben asked Amy.

"Well, he really injured his spine and was in a wheel-chair for a bit," Amy explained. "He did get better, but the doctors said that it would be too dangerous for him to ever ride again." Her voice hardened. "It was really hard on him, and he couldn't cope with the situation, and so he ran off, abandoning us and the horses. He didn't want anything to do with us or his old life anymore, so Mom decided to move back here to live with Grandpa."

"Come on, Amy. That's not true!"

Amy turned. Lou was staring angrily at her. "Dad did try to get back together with Mom. And you know it. Did you forget about that letter? It's proof that he just needed time."

There was no way Amy could have forgotten the

letter. It had been a real shock when she and Lou had found the note from their dad, begging their mom for a reconciliation. They had found it while clearing out Marion's room.

Lou's blue eyes flashed. "If Mom had stayed in England instead of running off to the States, then maybe there's a chance that they *would* have gotten back together!"

"You don't know that," Amy said hotly. "And what was Mom supposed to do? Wait around patiently until Dad decided he was ready to come back?"

"Yes! That's precisely what she should have done!" Lou exclaimed.

"Amy! Lou!" Jack Bartlett said, stepping forward. "That's enough!" His voice softened. "I know both of you have strong feelings, but a lot of stuff went on at the time that neither of you know about. Don't judge your parents now."

Lou turned abruptly and went back to the sink. Amy knew that her sister didn't feel the same about their father as she did. Devastated by his disappearance, Lou had refused to accept that he wasn't coming back. When Marion had told them of her plans to move back to Virginia, she had refused to go, begging to be allowed to stay at her English boarding school instead. When their mom had been alive, Lou had made it abundantly clear that she saw the move to Virginia as a betrayal of their father.

Ben cleared his throat. "So your mom came here to live?" he said, breaking the silence.

Amy spoke more quietly. "Yeah, my mom and I came here with Pegasus. He was emotionally traumatized, and conventional medicine was only helping his physical wounds, so my mom began to explore alternative therapies. When Pegasus recovered, Mom started Heartland to put the methods she had learned into practice — with the aim of helping other horses."

"And your mom never competed again?" Ben asked.

"No, she was far more interested in her work here."

"What about you, Amy?" Ben asked, sitting down. "Do you show?"

"Occasionally," Amy replied. "When I get the time, I take Sundance, my pony, in the Large Pony Hunter division."

"How about you, Ty?" Ben asked.

"No," Ty said. "I'm not interested."

"Not at all?" Ben said, looking surprised.

Ty shook his head. "I've had a few people ask me to take their horses in classes, but competing doesn't really do it for me. I think working with damaged horses is more satisfying."

Amy smiled at Ty, knowing just how he felt.

Ben didn't look as if he understood them at all. "I just couldn't be like that," he said, shaking his head. "I mean, how do you prove that you're really good at what you do? I love the thrill of competing and putting in a really good ride. It's great to get the ribbon and know that everyone has seen you do your best."

Ty shrugged. "I guess I just don't care that much about what other people think."

For a moment, Ty and Ben's eyes met, and Amy felt a certain tension creep into the air.

"OK, guys," Jack Bartlett announced. "Dinner's ready."

With the sudden bustle of movement, the tension dissolved. Chair legs scraped as they all sat down, and Lou began to hand out platefuls of baked ham, a basket of cornbread, and a bowl heaped with black-eyed peas.

"This looks incredible," Ben said, helping himself.

"I'd like to propose a toast to the latest addition to Heartland," Jack said, lifting his glass when everyone's plate was piled high. "Welcome, Ben," he said. "And I hope you have a very happy time here."

They all raised their glasses. "To Ben!" they echoed.

Ben raised his glass back with an easy smile. "To Heartland," he said.

❧

When Amy's alarm clock rang as usual at six o'clock the next morning, she hit the off button with a groan.

She hadn't gone to bed until after midnight, and the last thing she felt like doing right now was leaping up to face the day. However, the horses, as always, were waiting.

Yawning, she climbed out of bed, and with eyes half closed pulled on her jeans. Not bothering to brush her long hair, she went downstairs and slipped on her boots.

Going out into the yard, she thought about Ben. He had been a fun guest to have over for dinner. He had talked to Lou about her old job in Manhattan and to Grandpa about his farming days. Amy had even managed to find out that he wasn't dating anyone — a piece of information that she knew would please Soraya tremendously.

She refilled the water buckets and had just started to mix the feeds when Ty arrived. "Morning," he said, coming into the feed room. "Any sign of Ben yet?"

Amy shook her head as she added scoopfuls of soaked beet pulp to the grain in the buckets. "No." Ben was supposed to start work at seven o'clock, the same as Ty, but he hadn't arrived. "He'll probably be here any minute," she said.

However, Ben's truck didn't appear until more than an hour later. Hearing the engine, Amy looked out of Sundance's stall.

"Hi, there!" Ben said, jumping out of the truck. "Great morning, isn't it?" he said enthusiastically.

Amy had expected him to be full of apologies for being so late. "Yeah, I guess so," she replied.

Ben seemed to sense her reserve. "Hey, sorry I'm a little late," he said. "You don't mind, do you? I overslept. I guess I'm just tired from yesterday's move."

"It's OK," Amy said, pushing down the little voice in her head that was suggesting that maybe an hour and a half was more than a *little* late.

"OK, then," Ben said. "What do you want me to do?"

"I guess I should show you where things are first," Amy said. "And then you can help Ty and me. We've already finished the feeding and are mucking out the stalls. Then we sweep the barns and groom and exercise until lunchtime. Come on, I'll introduce you to the horses."

"Hang on a sec," Ben said. "I just want to say hi to Red."

Amy waited patiently as Ben went up to the tall chestnut and patted him and spoke to him in a quiet voice. Amy watched the horse nuzzle Ben's shoulder. He obviously adored his owner.

Ben joined her after a few minutes, and she began to take him around the stalls. "This is Jake," she said, stroking the bay Clydesdale in the stall next to Red's. "He's twenty-one." Jake pushed hopefully against her hand, and taking the hint, she fished out a packet of mints from her pocket. "Mom rescued him at a horse sale," Amy explained. "He has really bad arthritis and can't be rehomed."

"How many horses do you have here?" Ben asked.

"There are seven boarders and ten rescue horses," Amy said. "Eight of the rescues will hopefully recover enough so we can find them new homes. Two of them are here permanently — Jake and my pony, Sundance." She kissed Jake's nose. "I hate saying good-bye to horses when they leave. You get so attached to them." She glanced at Ben to see if he understood, but he was moving on to the next stall.

"That's Gypsy Queen," she said, going after him. "She's here to be cured of her bucking habit." She was about to explain more about Gypsy's history and her owner, but Ben was already walking to the next stall.

He showed a similar lack of interest when Amy started to tell him about the different therapies they used at Heartland. She showed him the medicine cabinet filled with her mom's books, herbal treatments, aromatherapy oils, and Bach Flower Remedies.

"What's the point of all this?" Ben said at last. "I mean, why not just trust the vet?"

"We do," Amy said. "It's just that Mom believed that you can use natural remedies to complement traditional medicine. Our vet, Scott, pretty much agrees." She saw the skeptical look on Ben's face. "Our methods *do* work, you know. Don't forget, we cured your aunt's horse, Promise, when nobody else managed to."

"I suppose," Ben said, but he still looked less than convinced. He stepped toward the door. "You said the stalls need finishing off. Should I get started? Ty looked like he could use some help."

Amy nodded and Ben strode off.

Amy stared after him, feeling confused. Lisa was paying for Ben to be at Heartland, but he didn't seem at all interested in their work — in fact, he acted like he didn't even think their methods could help.

✎

When they stopped for lunch, Ben got out his grooming kit and tack. "Aren't you going to eat?" Amy asked. "We still have ham for sandwiches."

"I'm going to ride first," Ben replied, heading in the direction of Red's stall.

"So what do you think of him now?" Amy asked Ty as they went into the kitchen.

"What — apart from him being an hour and a half late, taking two hours to muck out four stalls, and not showing any interest in the work we do here?" Ty replied dryly.

Amy smiled. "Yeah, despite that. What do you think?"

Ty shrugged. "I don't know. It'll probably take him time to adjust. Ask me in a week or so."

As Amy made herself a sandwich, she looked out the window and saw Ben walking Red up the path to the schooling ring. "Want to sit outside and watch him ride?" she said.

Ty nodded and, taking their lunch with them, they headed toward the training ring.

Ben was cantering Red in a figure eight. With light and fluid movements, the chestnut executed a perfect flying change in the center of the ring. Amy saw Ben stroke Red's neck, his lips moving in praise as they cantered on, his body still in the saddle, his back straight, and his hands maintaining light, steady contact with the horse's mouth.

"They look good," she said in a low voice to Ty.

Seemingly oblivious to their presence, Ben turned Red down the center of the ring, steering to where there was a four-foot jump. With barely a change in his stride pattern, Red approached and cleared it as easily as if it had been a fence half the height. To Amy, watching at the gate, the bond between horse and rider was unmistakable, but at the same time, she had to question whether Red was warmed up properly before Ben started jumping him.

As Ben cantered past, he seemed to notice them for

the first time. In one easy transition, he brought Red from a canter to a walk. "Hey," he said, circling Red back toward them.

"Hi," Ty replied.

"You jumped that well," Amy said.

Ben smiled. "Thanks." He patted Red. "I thought I might take him out on a trail ride for a bit. Do either of you feel like coming? It would help to have someone show me the trails around here."

"Sure, I'll come out on Sundance," Amy said. She glanced at Ty. "How about it, Ty? Are you going to come?"

"I'd better not," Ty said. "Solo, Charlie, and Moochie need working in the ring, and there is a lot of grooming to do."

"You're right." Amy felt guilty. "Maybe I should stay."

"No, it's OK. You go," Ty said. "Ben needs someone who knows the trails, and Sundance could use the exercise."

"Great, it's settled, then," Ben said, looking at Amy. "I'll walk Red around and cool him off while you get ready."

"Are you sure you don't mind?" Amy asked Ty as Ben walked Red away.

"It's fine," Ty replied. "You just go ahead and enjoy yourself," he teased. "Don't worry about me. I'll stay and do all the work — as usual."

"That's right," Amy said with a grin. "I never do any-thing around here."

"You said it." Ty said, dodging quickly as she swung a playful punch at him.

As Amy walked to the ponies' turnout field to catch Sundance, she felt another flicker of guilt. Now that they had so many horses boarding, Ty was working harder than ever — he was working until late in the evening and never taking his days off. *Oh, well*, she thought as she reached the paddock gate and called to Sundance, *hopefully now that Ben's here to help, things should start getting easier for him — for both of us.*

It only took Amy five minutes to run a brush over Sundance's coat and tack up. She mounted and went up to the ring. "I'm ready."

"Great," Ben said. "Let's go."

They rode out of the yard to Teak's Hill, the wooded mountain that rose up behind Heartland. Just before the trail left the fields and entered the trees, Amy stopped Sundance. "I love this view," she said, looking at Heartland stretched out below them, the barns and paddocks bathed in the glow of the October sun.

"It's beautiful up here," Ben said, looking around.

"Your aunt's barn is great, too," Amy said. "It must have been amazing to grow up there."

"Yeah," Ben said, with the hint of a dry, unamused laugh. "I guess it was."

Amy glanced at him.

Ben gathered up his reins. "So what are we waiting for?" he said, trotting Red on. "I thought you were supposed to be showing me around."

Amy trotted after him. Patches of sunlight filtered through the treetops and dappled the shady track. "That leads up to Clairdale Ridge," Amy said, pointing out the trail as they rode past it. "And the trail we're going to take up here on the left leads down to the creek."

They approached the fallen tree that Sundance had jumped the day before. Seeing it, the buckskin's ears pricked forward.

"Can we jump that?" Ben asked. "Is it safe?"

"Yeah, it's fine," Amy said, holding Sundance back. She let Ben go first and watched as he cantered Red toward the tree trunk. As he neared it, the young horse spooked at the unfamiliar jump and stopped.

Amy gasped as Ben immediately brought his crop down on Red's neck. With a snort, the chestnut shot backward, head in the air. Clamping his legs on the horse's sides, Ben turned again toward the tree trunk. Amy saw the horse's ears prick forward in alarm and his stride shorten as his muscles tensed in defiance.

"Go on!" Ben said angrily, pounding his legs against Red's sides.

"Ben! He's scared!" Amy exclaimed as the chestnut began to back away from the trunk.

"He has to learn," Ben shouted back.

Amy cantered over. "Don't upset him. I can give you a lead on Sundance if you want," she appealed in a calm voice.

Ben ignored her. Using his heels and his seat, he urged Red forward. The horse took two short strides and plunged toward the trunk. Ben brought his crop down on the horse's shoulder, and Red took off in a massive leap. As they landed on the other side, Ben patted Red's shoulder and praised him. "Good boy!" He turned triumphantly to Amy. "See? He had to learn there was nothing to be afraid of."

But did he have to learn that way? Amy thought, looking at the sweat that had broken out on the chestnut's neck. She wanted to tell Ben that scolding a horse to overcome fear is not a good way to build trust. However, she bit back the words. Seeing Ben pat Red now, she knew that he hadn't meant to be cruel. He obviously just used different methods from those she used — the kind of forceful methods that most of the horse world used. But Amy couldn't figure out why anyone would train with force when you could accomplish just as much — even more — through cooperation and understanding.

"There are other ways to get a horse to do what you

want," she said to Ben. Clicking her tongue, she cantered Sundance in a circle.

"You're not really going to jump it, are you?" Ben called in surprise. "Isn't it a bit big for him?"

Ignoring him, Amy turned Sundance toward the tree. His ears pricked up, his stride lengthened confidently, and in one smooth leap they were over.

"Way to go!" Ben exclaimed, looking very impressed. "For a pony, he sure can jump!"

Amy nodded as she trotted over. "He's won Large Pony Hunter Champion three times now. But I don't get many chances to show him. I'd like to try a few junior jumper classes, though."

"You should," Ben said. "With form like that, he'd have a great chance."

Amy patted Sundance, pleased at Ben's approval. "We rescued him from a sale. He probably would have been sold for glue if not for my mom and me," she said. "He was so bad tempered no one could cope with him. Now we get tons of offers for him. But I'll never let him go."

"I know how you feel," Ben said. He stroked Red's shoulder. "I'd never sell Red, either. No matter what anyone offered me."

Seeing Red turn and nuzzle Ben's hand, Amy began to forgive Ben for how he had behaved earlier.

She smiled back at Ben, and they continued along the track.

Ben patted Red. "I'm entered in a show next month with him. I thought I'd do a couple of classes to keep him going over the winter and then take the circuit seriously next summer." He looked at Amy. "We could do some shows together. My trailer takes up to three horses. You could really go for it with Sundance, too."

Amy was flattered, but she shook her head. "Thanks, but I couldn't be away from Heartland for that long."

"You know it's a waste," Ben said. "You could be really good."

Amy shrugged. "Heartland's more important to me than competing."

"Nothing's more important to me than competing," Ben said, his voice suddenly sounding determined. Shortening his reins, he leaned forward in his saddle. "Come on, I'll race you to the bend in the track!"

Chapter Three

When Amy and Ben got back to Heartland, Ty was riding Moochie. "We'd better get back to the grooming," Amy said.

"Sure," Ben replied. "I'll be with you as soon as I've put Red away."

Amy thought that Ben meant that he would just give Red a quick rubdown before returning him to his stall. However, it was almost an hour before he eventually reappeared. "OK, who do you want me to start on?" he asked.

Amy was just finishing Jasmine. There were only three horses left to groom. "Can you do Jake and Sugarfoot?" she said, feeling slightly irritated that he'd been gone so long.

Ben nodded cheerfully and fetched a grooming kit.

When he came back, Amy was just going into Dancer's stall. "This is Dancer, right?" Ben said.

Amy nodded.

Ben stepped into the stall and reached to pat Dancer's neck, but he moved too quickly, and the mare reacted like lightning. Throwing her head up with a squeal, she snapped at Ben's arm.

"Hey!" Ben shouted, smacking her in the jaw.

"Ben! No!" Amy cried in horror, grabbing his arm.

It was too late. Dancer's eyes flashed with white, and she started kicking in fear.

"Get out!" Amy cried, brushing past Ben and yanking on his arm.

She dragged him out of the stall and shut the door just as Dancer's hooves smashed into the side wall. Almost beside herself with anger, she turned to Ben. "How could you do that!" she cried. "Dancer's scared enough of people as it is!"

Ben stared at her. "But she tried to bite me!"

"So? We don't *hit* horses here."

"You mean you just let them bite?" Ben exclaimed. "That's crazy! How will they ever learn to respect you if you let them get away with things like that?"

Amy's gray eyes flashed. "You don't need to hit a horse to get it to respect you. Especially a horse like Dancer, who has been abused."

"So what *do* you do?" Ben said. "She's not going to stop biting on her own."

"If you treat them with the respect they deserve, show them understanding, and let them realize that there is nothing to be afraid of, you'll be surprised how some horses will change. Have you seen the scars on Dancer's head?" Amy demanded. "They're from a halter being on so tight that her skin was rubbed raw. That halter was left on for more than a year. Of course she tried to bite you when you put your hand up to her head like that. You'd have done the same. You can't blame her."

Ben looked slightly ashamed. "I didn't realize." He looked at the mare, now standing trembling at the back of her stall. "Hey, I'm sorry if I scared her."

Amy took a deep breath to try to control her anger. "Look, just make sure you remember that we never hit any of the horses here. Every single one of them is damaged in some way. What we need to do is gain their trust, not frighten them even more."

Ben swallowed hard. "OK, I get it." He looked at Dancer again. "Is there anything you can do to calm her down?"

"I'll see," Amy said. Leaving the halter on the floor, she walked quietly into the stall. Dancer stared at her warily.

"It's OK, girl," Amy told her softly, feeling in her pocket for the packet of mints and offering her one. "I won't hurt you."

Dancer watched Amy for a moment and then stepped forward cautiously, her neck outstretched, her brown-and-white nostrils blowing in and out. Amy let the mare snuffle the mint up from her hand and then moved quietly to stand beside her shoulder. Dancer shifted uneasily in the straw. Very gently, still speaking soothingly to the frightened horse, Amy put her hand lightly on Dancer's shoulder and began to move her fingers in a series of small circles, each circle moving on to a new patch of skin.

Forgetting about Ben watching from the doorway, she concentrated totally on the mare. As the minutes passed, she felt the horse's muscles begin to relax slightly, and Amy slowed the circles down, moving them gradually up Dancer's neck toward her head. Every time the mare tensed, she lightened her touch, but gradually Dancer started to relax more and more until she was allowing Amy to work tiny circles over her muzzle, nostrils, and lips.

As Amy worked, the mare yawned and slowly lowered her head, her eyes half closing. At last, Amy stopped, and moving quietly to the door, she picked up the halter and slipped it over Dancer's nose.

Dancer didn't even flinch. Buckling it up, Amy led the now calm mare toward the front of the stall.

"That's amazing," Ben said in surprise. "She's OK now just because of a massage?"

"It's not really massage," Amy explained. "It's a form of therapy called T-touch." She tied Dancer up. "See? Force isn't the best way to get a horse to do what you want."

Ben frowned. "I get your point with horses like Dancer," he said. "But a regular horse responds to discipline. Look at Red. I'm firm with him, but you would never say that he's scared of me, and we work great together."

"But why use force when you can get a horse to work just as well without it?" Amy asked.

Ben shrugged. "It's just what I've always done. Red and I have a lot of training to do. He has a lot to learn about being a jumper, and we've got a system that works for us." Ben saw Amy's face. "Look, don't worry, I'll respect your rules with Heartland's horses. Just don't expect me to change what I do with Red." He picked up the grooming kit again. "Now, I'd better get started grooming that Shetland — Sugarfoot, right?"

Amy nodded and started to brush Dancer. She didn't know what to make of Ben. He seemed so skeptical. He was not at all prepared to accept Heartland's methods and ideas, and yet he was obviously a good rider and completely devoted to Red. Amy didn't think he needed to resort to crops and harsh treatment to train his horse. She thought that over time she and Ty would be able to persuade him to change his ideas. She patted Dancer. She hoped she was right.

✐

At five o'clock, Amy and Ty started to fill the evening hay nets. They were running late as usual. "At least all the horses have been exercised," Amy said to Ty as they stuffed sweet-smelling meadow hay into the nets.

"Yeah, and with three of us we should be able to stack the rest of the hay delivery in the feed room in no time," Ty said. "That's if we all put our backs into it."

Just then, there was the sound of footsteps. Ben looked over the door. "I'm finished grooming, so I'll be heading out."

Amy stared at him. "Going? But we haven't fed the horses yet."

"I'm off at five," Ben said in surprise.

Amy was at a loss for words. He was right of course. But working with horses wasn't like a regular job; you didn't just leave when your hours were up.

"I usually stay 'til things are done," Ty said pointedly.

"Great," Ben said cheerfully. "If you're staying, then I'm OK to go, right?"

"Well, actually, Ben, if you could stick around until the feeds are done, it would help a lot," Amy said quickly, seeing that he hadn't taken the hint.

Ben looked taken aback. "I guess I could."

"Good," Amy said, feeling awkward that she had to ask. "You could start mixing the feeds, and we'll finish these nets off."

Ben did as Amy suggested. As they heard the rattle of the buckets being put out on the floor, Amy and Ty exchanged glances. They continued filling the hay nets in silence.

At last the horses were fed. "See you tomorrow," Ben said.

Amy nodded, not able to bring herself to mention that the hay delivery still needed to be dealt with.

She watched Ben drive off. "Well," she said to Ty. "I don't know what to think of that."

"I guess he's used to his aunt's barn. They probably have enough staff to get everything done during normal working hours," Ty said.

Amy thought about Lisa Stillman's immaculate breeding stable with its army of stable hands and thought Ty must be right. "It's gotta be a big change for him. Ben's probably not even used to cleaning stalls and doing things like that."

Ty looked at her. "Well, you think he'll get used to it here?"

Amy remembered what had happened earlier that afternoon. "I'm sure he will," she said, trying to be positive. "It'll just take time."

For a moment, Ty didn't say anything, but then he nodded. "Well, we'll just wait and see."

ᘒᕒ

Ben didn't arrive the next morning until Amy was going into the house to get changed for school. She didn't have time to ask why he was late. She hardly had a chance to think about it. School mornings were always hectic, and as usual, none of her school stuff was organized. She showered in two minutes flat, pulled on some clean clothes, and raced downstairs.

"What about breakfast, Amy?" her grandpa said despairingly, as she grabbed her sneakers and started to pull them on.

"I don't have time!" Amy said. "I'll miss the bus!"

"But Amy, you can't go without breakfast," Jack Bartlett said.

"Why do we have to go through this every morning?" Lou said from the kitchen table. "Why don't you get your stuff together the night before and come in from the barn at a decent time?"

"Here, take this," her grandpa said, shoving a muffin into Amy's hand.

"Thanks, Grandpa!" Amy said, giving him a kiss as she slung her backpack over her shoulder. "See you later. Bye, Lou!"

With that, she ran out of the house.

Ty was standing by the tap filling up a water bucket. "Have a good day," he called.

"Like that's going to happen," Amy said, pausing briefly. "I've got two periods of math first thing."

Ty grinned. "Better you than me."

"See you later!" said Amy, jogging off down the drive.

She made it to the stop just as the bus arrived. Soraya had saved a seat beside her. "So, come on — tell me all the gossip about Ben," she said as Amy sat down.

"Well, he's not very good at being on time," Amy said as she caught her breath. "He's been late both mornings since he got here."

"And you're *never* late," Soraya grinned, looking at Amy's flushed face and disheveled hair.

Amy grinned back. "OK, OK."

"Did you find out if he has a girlfriend?" Soraya asked.

"Yes," Amy said. "And he doesn't."

"Now *that* really is interesting," Soraya said slowly. "So how's he fitting in at Heartland?"

As Amy started to tell her all about Ben she noticed that the girl sitting in a seat across the aisle kept looking at her. "Who's that?" Amy whispered to Soraya when the girl looked away.

"I don't know," Soraya replied. "Maybe she's new."

The girl glanced at them again. She had short brown hair and a heart-shaped face.

"Hi," Soraya said, smiling in her usual friendly way.

The girl turned red. "Oh . . . hi," she said nervously.

"Did you just start at Jefferson High?" Soraya asked, leaning forward.

The girl nodded. "Yes. My name's Claire Whitely."

"We thought you might be new," Soraya said. "Where are you from?"

"Philadelphia," the girl said. "We moved here because of my mom's job."

"Well, I'm Soraya Martin, and this is Amy Fleming," Soraya told her. "If you want to know anything about school, just ask us."

Amy nodded.

"Thanks," Claire said. Her cheeks became a bit pinker. "Actually, I couldn't help overhearing your conversation," she said, looking at Amy. "Do you — do you live at Heartland?"

"Yeah," Amy replied, feeling surprised.

Claire's blue eyes widened. "I read about Heartland in an issue of *Horse Life*. It sounds amazing. I knew it was somewhere in Virginia, but I had no idea it was *here*."

"Do you ride?" Amy asked her.

"Yeah," Claire said shyly. "My dad just bought me my own horse. My parents are divorced, and he just left to go work in Europe for a few months. So he gave me Flint before he left — that's my horse. He's a Thorough-bred."

"That's a pretty nice gift!" Soraya said.

Clare nodded. "I've wanted a horse forever. I think my dad feels bad that I don't get to see him much. But Flint's just brilliant. He was really expensive, but he's won a lot of awards, so he must be worth it."

Looking at the glow in Claire's eyes as she talked about Flint, Amy forgave her for bragging a bit. She just seemed so excited to have her own horse.

Claire looked at her and swallowed. "Would you — would you like to come and see him?" she asked hesitantly. "You, too, Soraya. You could come after school today. I'm going to the stable anyway. But you don't have to unless you want to," she added hurriedly.

"No, I'd like to see him," Amy said.

"Me, too," Soraya said.

"You would?" Claire looked as if she could hardly believe it.

Amy nodded. "Where is your stable?"

"Green Briar," Claire replied eagerly. "Do you know it?"

Amy and Soraya's eyes met. They knew it all too well. Green Briar was a large hunter/jumper barn that specialized in producing push-button horses and ponies that always racked in the ribbons. The stable was run by Val Grant. Her daughter, Ashley, was in the same class as Amy and Soraya at school, and whenever Amy took

Sundance to local shows, Ashley was one of Amy's fiercest rivals.

"Yeah, we know it," Soraya replied dryly.

"Great," Claire said, oblivious to the look that had passed between them. "Do you want to come by this afternoon?"

"I have to go home first and make sure everything's OK," Amy said. "But we could meet you there." She didn't particularly want to go to Green Briar, but she thought it would be nice to be friendly with Claire, and it would be interesting to see Flint.

"OK," Claire said, her eyes shining. "That would be great."

❧

School seemed to drag by that day. All Amy could think about was whether Ben and Ty were getting along at Heartland and how things would go when she and Soraya went to see Claire's horse. Soraya phoned her mom at lunchtime, and Mrs. Martin agreed to give them a ride to Green Briar.

"See you later," Amy said to Soraya and Claire as she got off the bus.

"Yeah, bye," they called.

Amy hurried up Heartland's winding drive. When she reached the top, she saw Ty coming out of the tack room. "Hi," she said, going over to him. "How's it been today?"

"Busy," Ty said. "But almost everyone has been worked. There's just Ivy and Solo left."

"I'll do them," Amy offered. "But do you mind if I go over to Green Briar first?"

"Green Briar?" Ty echoed. "What do you want to go there for?"

Amy told Ty about Flint. "I'd like to see him, and Soraya's mom said she'd drive us. It shouldn't take long."

"That's fine," Ty said. "I'll get Ben to help sweep — when he's finished riding Red."

"He's riding Red?" Amy said, surprised that Ben was riding his own horse when there was still work to be done.

Ty nodded. "Yeah. And he rode him for an hour this morning." He looked concerned. "Don't you think two workouts is a lot for a young horse?"

"Well, Ben did say that he's got a show next month," Amy said. "And lots of competition horses get ridden twice a day."

"Yeah, but they don't normally jump three-foot courses each time," Ty said. "I could understand him riding once in the ring and once on the trails, but he did heavy work, and he rode more than an hour both times."

Amy frowned. Ty was right. Two hour-long training

sessions was a lot of work for any horse, let alone a young horse like Red.

"And it's not like there wasn't anything else to do," Ty added.

Amy nodded. "Maybe we should talk with him later."

She went to get changed. As she came out of the house, Ben was walking Red down the path from the training ring. "Hi!" he called, catching sight of her and stopping Red. "He's been great today."

Amy didn't know what to say. She wanted to yell at him for jumping Red twice that day and not helping Ty more, but she didn't know how to start. And she didn't think it would be right. It was a tricky situation when his aunt was paying for him to be there. Under any other circumstance she wouldn't have hesitated to speak out and let her thoughts be known, but this was different.

"Good," she said. "I, er, think Ty could use a hand in the barn."

"Sure," Ben said. "I'll just cool Red down first."

"OK, but don't take too long," Amy said sharply.

Ben looked surprised.

Just then, the Martins' car came up the drive, and Amy realized that the conversation with Ben would have to wait.

"Hi, Ben," Soraya said, getting out of the car.

Ben smiled at her. "Hi. How are you doing?"

"Great," Soraya said with a smile.

Seeing that Soraya looked as if she was about to start a conversation, Amy grabbed her arm. They didn't want to be late for Claire. "Hello, Mrs. Martin," she said as she pulled Soraya into the back of the car.

"Hi, Amy," Mrs. Martin replied, turning the car around.

"Did you see the way Ben smiled at me?" Soraya said with a giggle. "He is *so* cute!"

"Soraya Martin!" her mom said, overhearing. "I thought you liked going to Heartland because of the horses."

"I do!" Soraya protested. "Besides, Ben just started working there."

But then, shooting Amy a sideways look that her mom couldn't see, she grinned.

Amy smiled back at her friend, but inwardly she was worried by the situation with Ben.

∾

Claire was waiting for them in the paved parking lot at Green Briar. "Flint's stall is in that barn over there," she said, leading them across the immaculate yard toward a spacious modern barn. They passed a large, all-weather training ring where three beautiful horses were being schooled over a line of fences. In the middle of the ring stood Val Grant. With a cell phone clipped onto the back of her tight maroon breeches and a lunge whip in her hand, she called out instructions to the riders. Amy hurried past, not wanting to be seen. If she could see Flint and get away from Green Briar without having to talk to Val Grant or Ashley, she would be amazingly relieved. She cringed as there was a rattle of poles, and she heard Val Grant's voice yell out in strident tones, "What do you think your crop's for, Yvonne? Use it!"

Amy exchanged looks with Soraya as they hurried into the barn.

"That's him," Claire said. "Five stalls down on the left. The dark gray."

Amy looked down the row of stalls to where a beautiful iron-gray Thoroughbred was looking over his half door. His elegant ears were pricked, his brown eyes were large and thoughtful.

"He's very handsome," Amy said, going over. "Hi, boy."

Flint looked at her with an odd expression on his face.

Amy peered over the stall door. He was a fantastic-looking horse, very athletic with strong, clean legs and a noble head.

Soraya and Claire joined her. "He *is* handsome, isn't he?" Claire said, waiting for their approval.

"He sure is," Soraya said.

Amy nodded in agreement. "Are you going to ride him?" she asked.

Claire seemed suddenly hesitant. "Ummm, well, I don't know."

"Oh, you've got to!" Soraya said.

"OK," Claire agreed slowly. "I'll get my tack."

A few minutes later, Claire returned with her saddle and bridle. Her fingers fumbled with the bolt as she let herself into the stall. As she moved toward Flint, he tossed his head into the air.

"Steady, boy," Claire said, her voice sounding nervous.

Flint sidestepped away from her and moved to the back of his stall so his hindquarters were pointing in Claire's direction. Putting his ears back, Flint lifted one back hoof and stamped it on the ground. Claire jumped back quickly.

"Is he always like this?" Soraya asked.

"Not always, but most of the time," Claire said, grateful for the excuse to step back to the door. "He was OK at first, but he's been getting worse. Sometimes it can take me almost an hour to brush him and tack up."

Amy stared at her in astonishment. "An hour!"

"He just keeps lifting his back foot at me like that," Claire said, her face turning red. "I'm not sure what to do."

Amy frowned. She had seen the way Flint had been watching Claire as he stood in the corner, his ears pricked, his eyes bright. He didn't look mean. In fact, she had a strong feeling that he was just taking advantage of Claire's lack of experience. "Here, do you want me to try?" she said.

Claire gratefully handed her the bridle.

Ignoring the way Flint lifted his back hoof from the floor, Amy marched around to his head, grabbed his mane so that he couldn't swing away, and deftly tossed the reins over his head. "Got you!" she said. Taking hold of his nose, she slipped the bit in his mouth and pulled the headpiece over his ears. Flint looked at her determined face and didn't object.

"I think you're going to have to be a bit firmer with him," she said to Claire. "He's just being difficult."

She finished tacking Flint up and then led him outside and handed the reins to Claire.

Claire glanced at the main training ring. Val Grant was still working with the three riders. "We'll take him to the back ring," she said quickly.

Amy and Soraya followed her around to a smaller training ring behind the barns. Claire led Flint in through the gate and then mounted.

As soon as she was in the saddle, Flint started to sidestep. "Steady," Claire said, her hands grabbing at the reins. Looking at Amy and Soraya, she tried to smile. "I'll just walk and trot him for a bit," she said.

As she rode off, Soraya turned to Amy. "She doesn't seem very confident," she said.

"I know," Amy said in a low voice as Flint jogged around the ring. Although Claire's position in the saddle was basically good, she was stiff and tense. "And he's quite a handful."

As they watched, Flint began to settle down, and Claire seemed to relax. But she didn't canter him.

After a bit, she rode Flint over to the gate. "He's great, isn't he?" she said proudly.

"Yeah," Amy agreed.

"But he does look like he could be high strung," Soraya said.

"That horse just needs someone in the saddle who can actually ride," a voice said behind them.

Amy swung round. Ashley Grant was standing there, arms crossed, platinum blond hair falling onto her shoulders.

"I told you, Flint's too much horse for a beginner like *you*," Ashley said to Claire. She shrugged. "But if you want, I guess I could spare the time to ride him and teach him a few things."

"Thanks, but I think I'll bring him in now," Claire said quickly. She hurriedly started to dismount. "He's done enough today."

Ashley laughed and turned to Amy. "So how's business at . . . Heartland?" she said, her eyebrows raising in an irritatingly mocking way as she said Heartland's name.

"Extremely busy, actually," Amy said coldly, moving to open the gate for Claire. "All our stalls are full, and we've got a new stable hand."

Ashley looked surprised. "What happened to Ty?"

"The new hand is in addition to Ty," Amy said as Claire led Flint out of the ring

Ashley crossed her arms. "You're never going to keep Ty, you know. He's good — even Mom says so. He could go places."

"He could, but he doesn't want to," Amy said.

"I wouldn't be so sure if I were you." Ashley said. "Does he know that we've just started looking for a new head groom? He might want to apply."

Amy laughed incredulously. "Get real, Ashley. Ty would never want to work somewhere like *here*."

Ashley looked round at the immaculate surroundings. "Oh, really? So Ty wouldn't want to work at a stable with three training rings, a cross-country course, three state-of-the-art barns, efficient staff, and top-quality horses? Think about it, Amy," she said sarcastically. "Working here is every stable hand's dream. Particularly when you think of what Ty puts up with instead — one run-down stable with two dinky barns, two small rings, and a bunch of horses that no one wants."

Amy longed to say something clever back, but the truth in Ashley's words hit home. "Ty wouldn't come here!" she said, desperately wanting to reassure herself, but she was feeling less convinced.

"Mom would pay a lot to get someone like him," Ashley said. "Maybe I'll tell her to give him a call," she added casually.

"Do whatever you want!" Amy exclaimed, feeling her temper start to rise. "But Ty won't leave Heartland!"

Ashley's lips curved into an mischievous smile. "Oh, really?" she said. Her green eyes challenged Amy. "Well, I guess we'll just have to see about that."

Chapter Four

Amy was still furious with Ashley when Mrs. Martin dropped her off at Heartland half an hour later. She was sure that Ty wouldn't leave Heartland. Soraya had tried to reassure her, but Ashley had lodged a nagging doubt in her mind. Amy couldn't imagine how much Val Grant would offer Ty to steal him away. Whatever it was, Amy knew that Lou would never be able to match it. Extra money was something they didn't have at Heartland. And what about the opportunities he'd have at Green Briar? It was four times as big as Heartland.

Amy pushed away the questions. She was being ridiculous. Ty loved Heartland. She told herself that she knew him well enough to realize he would never consider leaving.

As she walked across the yard she saw Ben coming out of Red's stall. "Hi," he said.

Amy remembered that she had been planning to talk to him some more. She went over, wondering how to begin. "He's in great condition," she said, patting Red's muscular neck.

Ben nodded. "Yeah. I ride him twice a day."

"Isn't that a bit much for a young horse?" Amy said, trying to get the conversation around to what she wanted to talk about.

Ben shook his head. "If I want to make it to the top he needs to be fit."

"Yeah, but you don't need to school him twice a day," Amy said. "Ty said you jumped him both times you rode today. He was a little concerned."

"What does he know?" Ben said, looking angry. "He doesn't even ride competitively."

"He knows a lot!" Amy said, jumping to Ty's defense. "And he only mentioned it because he was worried about Red."

"Well, I don't need him to look out for my horse!" Ben said defiantly. "I know what's best for Red." He looked at her and changed his expression. "You should appreciate the demands of training a top competition horse, Amy. You saw your mom and dad do it."

Amy didn't want to get into a huge fight with Ben on only his second day. "I guess," she said, reluctantly backing down. She guessed that he had done the same at Fairfield, and Lisa Stillman had felt it was reasonable training for a show horse.

Just then the phone rang. "I'll get it!" Amy heard Ty yell as he came out of the tack room.

Five minutes later, he walked back toward the barn. Amy was filling Jake's water bucket. "Who was it?" she called.

Ty walked toward her, his dark eyes amused. "You will *never* guess."

"I have no idea," Amy said, shaking her head.

"It was Val Grant," Ty said. "And she just offered me a job at Green Briar." He had a huge grin on his face.

Amy was stunned. "Val Grant!"

Ty took in her expression and burst out laughing. "I'm not sure why she asked me. She hadn't said more than two words to me before," he said, shaking his head.

"What did you say?" Amy asked with concern.

"What do you mean?" Ty said, looking at Amy. "It's not really my thing. I mean, the money would be better, and it would be cool to be head groom, but I don't think it's a good move. She just doesn't see things the same way that I do."

"What?" Amy said sarcastically. "Val Grant, who would have a crop surgically attached to her arm if possible, doesn't see things like you?"

"Exactly," Ty said with a laugh and a smile, and then turned back toward the tack room.

Amy felt better knowing Ty wasn't really considering it, but some of her concern still lingered. She and Ty could joke all they wanted, but Amy knew it was a serious matter. If Ty left, it would change everything.

❧

That night, as the family sat down to dinner, Lou asked how Ben was settling in.

Amy didn't know what to say.

"There isn't a problem, is there, Amy?" Grandpa said, seeing her hesitate.

"No . . . no, he's OK," Amy said, reaching out for the water pitcher.

Jack Bartlett frowned. "Just OK?" Amy could tell that he thought she was trying to hide something. "Amy, what's on your mind?"

"Nothing." Amy saw her grandpa's eyebrows rise. "It's just that he's got some different ideas than we have," she tried to explain. "But I don't think it'll be a major problem."

Just then the phone rang.

"I'll get it!" Amy said, glad for the distraction. She jumped up and grabbed the receiver. "Heartland, Amy Fleming speaking."

"Hi, Amy. It's Scott."

Hearing the familiar voice of their local vet, Amy smiled. "Hey, Scott."

Scott cleared his throat. "Is Lou there?" he asked.

"Yeah," Amy said, nodding. "Let me get her." She held the cordless phone out to her sister. "It's Scott," she said, grinning.

Lou's cheeks turned pink. "For me?"

"Yes," Amy replied, her eyes glinting teasingly at her sister. "For you."

Lou took the phone. "Hello, Scott?" she said, walking away from the table and turning her back to Amy. "Yes, I'm fine. How are you?"

Amy grinned at their grandpa as she sat back down, forgetting the conversation about Ben. "I bet Scott's going to ask Lou out on a date!" she said.

Jack Bartlett shook his head, but Amy saw him smile as he looked away. Although Grandpa would never say anything, she knew that he would be just as pleased as she would if Scott and Lou were to start dating. For the last couple of months — ever since Lou had broken up with her past boyfriend — she had become increasingly friendly with Scott. So far nothing had happened, but this was the first time that Scott had called just to talk to Lou.

Amy turned hopefully in her chair. She could just hear what Lou was saying. "I'd love to, Scott! That sounds great. OK, I'll see you then."

"Well?" Amy demanded as Lou put the phone down. "Did he ask you out?"

"Yes," Lou said, turning round and looking stunned. "He did. We're going out on Saturday."

"Oh, Lou! That's wonderful!" Amy cried, jumping to her feet and hugging her sister. "You and Scott are totally perfect for each other."

"It's only one date, Amy," Lou laughed, but despite her practical words her blue eyes sparkled.

❧

The next day on the school bus, Amy told Soraya the news. "Isn't it awesome?" she said.

"I wonder if Matt knows," Soraya said.

Matt was one of their best friends and Scott's younger brother. As soon as he got on the bus they told him.

"Cool," he said. He looked hopefully at Amy. "You know, we could always see if they want to make it a double date."

"Like they'll want us tagging along," Amy said.

"We could go somewhere else," Matt said.

"Oh, Matt. You know I'm just too busy with Heartland," Amy said. "Maybe another time."

Matt sighed theatrically. "Rejected again."

Amy grinned at him. "You'll get over it." Matt had been trying to persuade her to go out with him for almost a year now, but somehow she just couldn't see him as a boyfriend. She caught Soraya looking at her. She knew Soraya thought she was crazy to keep turning Matt down. He was cute, intelligent, popular, and great fun to be around.

"So who's the new girl you were talking to yesterday?" Matt said, glancing toward the front of the bus to where Claire was sitting.

"Claire Whitely," Amy replied.

"She just moved here from Philadelphia," Soraya said. "We went to see her horse yesterday. She's keeping it at Green Briar."

"How's she getting along with the Grants?" Matt said.

"She seemed a bit in awe of Ashley," Amy said, remembering the way Claire had stammered and turned red when Ashley had spoken to her.

"I don't blame her," Matt joked. "Ashley can be pretty intimidating."

Amy smiled. "Well, I think Claire's going to have to learn to stand up to her — if she plans to keep Flint at Green Briar, anyway."

"I feel bad for her," Soraya said genuinely. "It's bad enough seeing Ashley at school every day. Imagine having to see her after school as well." She nodded toward the front of the bus. "You know, she looks like something's wrong — I've been watching her."

Amy looked to the front of the bus. Claire was hugging her bag and looking out the window, obviously lost in thought.

When they arrived at school, Amy pushed forward to catch up with Claire as she got off the bus. "Hi. How are you?" she asked.

"Fine," Claire said quickly. Just then, Matt and a group of his friends jumped off the bus and pushed past them. One of their bags knocked against Claire's arm. "Ow!" she gasped, clutching her arm.

"What's the matter?" Amy demanded.

Claire bit her lip. She looked like she was struggling not to cry.

"Are you OK?" Soraya said, joining them and glancing at Claire, clutching her arm. "What's wrong?"

"It's my arm," Claire said. She moved to one side to let the rest of the students get by and then shrugged off her jacket. She was wearing a long-sleeved T-shirt underneath. When she rolled up the sleeve both Amy and Soraya gasped. On her upper arm there was a massive bruise. Black and deep purple, it radiated out from a pale imprint of teeth marks in the center.

"What happened?" Soraya asked.

Claire swallowed and pulled her jacket back on. "It was Flint," she said. "He bit me last night after you left."

"What did your mom say?" Amy asked.

"I haven't told her," Claire said. "And the worst thing

is, she's coming to watch me ride tonight. If he bites me when she's there, she'll want to get rid of him." Her eyes filled with tears. "She didn't want Daddy to buy him in the first place. She says I'm not ready to own a horse of my own."

Soraya glanced at Amy. "Maybe Amy could help. She's knows what to do with aggressive horses."

"Could you?" Claire said, hope lighting up her eyes as she looked at Amy.

Amy didn't know what to say. "Well, there's not much I can do while he's at Green Briar. Val Grant wouldn't be happy if she knew I was helping you at her stable." She saw Claire's face start to crumple and didn't know what to do. "Well, I could give you some advice on how to deal with him. And maybe I could come and help you tack him up tonight so that your mom doesn't see him being difficult. It's not going to solve the problem, but at least it will give you more time."

Claire nodded. "Oh, would you, please? If I can just stop Mom finding out, I'll work with him — I'll do whatever you say. I'm sure he'll get better."

"OK then. I'll come over right after school." Amy spoke lightly, but deep down she was worried. It was one thing for her to tell Claire what to do about Flint but quite another for Claire to carry out her instructions. From what Amy had seen of the Thoroughbred, it was clear that he needed an advanced rider, and nothing she could *say* was going to give Claire the experience she needed.

❧

When she got back to Heartland after school, Amy persuaded Grandpa to drive her over to Green Briar. "I'll be back in an hour," he said as he dropped her off outside the stately white gates.

"OK. See you later," Amy replied. As she walked through the gates, she saw Claire hurrying toward her.

"I'm so glad you're here. Mom will be here in about twenty minutes." She panted as she reached Amy. "And we've got to get him groomed and tacked up before then. But I warn you, he's acting pretty nasty."

Claire had already carried her grooming kit to Flint's stall. As she opened the door, he threw his head up and pinned his ears back. Claire hesitated. "That's a good boy," she said nervously. Flint stamped the ground and swished his tail. "That's what he was doing yesterday," Claire told Amy. She took a cautious step toward the horse. "Here, boy."

Flint swung his teeth at her, and Claire jumped back with a gasp.

Amy decided to take charge. She pushed past Claire. "That's enough!" she said sharply to Flint. He looked at her, his head held high, his eyes seeming to measure her up.

Amy took the halter from Claire and moved in swiftly beside Flint's head. In one quick movement, she pulled the halter over his nose and flicked the headpiece over his ears. As she went to buckle it up, he tossed his head up. "No!" she said. Flint looked at her and gave in.

Amy patted his neck and looked thoughtfully at his head. Her mom had always said you could tell a horse's personality by looking at its face. Flint had a slight moose nose, large eyes, and large, open nostrils. All of these attributes suggested that he was a highly intelligent horse. Amy looked at his ears. They were long and narrow — the sort of ears that were often found on horses that were difficult and temperamental. *Highly intelligent but difficult and temperamental,* Amy thought as she stroked Flint's straight nose. *Totally the wrong horse for a timid, unskilled rider.*

Amy's mom had taught her that most horses that were aggressive acted that way because they were scared. However, Amy was inclined to believe that Flint was one of the exceptions to this rule. She had a strong feeling that he was being aggressive with Claire simply because he thought he could get away with it. *And he's right,* she thought.

"What should I do with him, Amy?" Claire asked.

"You're just going to have to be firm," Amy said. She saw Claire's face. "I don't mean hit him, just firmly reprimand him when he misbehaves, and try not to be nervous." She began to tie Flint up. "We should get moving. Your mom will be here soon."

At first when Claire tried to help with the grooming, Flint swished his tail, but a firm word from Amy soon stopped his display of bad manners. "You've just got to let him know that you're in charge," she said.

At last, Flint was ready. They saddled him up and led him to the small training ring. As Claire put her foot in the stirrup, Flint danced on the spot. Claire tightened the reins nervously. "Stand." She tried to sound firm, but it didn't work. Her voice was too high and too faint. Flint sidestepped. Giving up trying to get him to stand still, Claire mounted and Flint started to walk before she was settled in the saddle.

Claire walked him around the ring. After one circuit, she let him trot. He pulled impatiently at the bit, with his head held high and his hindquarters sidling inward.

Suddenly, Flint caught sight of a cat running from under a pile of jumps at the end of the ring and spooked violently. He threw his head, and the sudden movement took Claire by surprise. She lost a stirrup and lost grip of the reins. Feeling the tension on his reins loosen, Flint thrust his head down and bucked three times.

"Hang on, Claire!" Amy cried from the gate.

Claire stayed on for the first buck, but as Flint's head went down between his knees for the second time, she lost her other stirrup and landed on his neck. The third buck sent her flying over his shoulder, and she crashed to the ground.

"Claire!" Amy exclaimed, her heart pounding as she scrambled over the gate.

But her voice was drowned out by a scream from behind her. "Claire! Oh, my goodness!"

Amy swung round. A woman with shoulder-length brown hair was rushing toward the gate.

"Mom!"

Amy looked back at Claire. She was sitting up, looking at the woman with horror in her eyes.

Chapter Five

Amy hesitated and then ran to the center of the ring. "Are you OK?" she demanded, reaching Claire.

To her relief, Claire nodded. "Yeah, I think so." Her voice trembled as she watched her mom opening the gate. "That's it, Amy. There's no way she'll let me keep him now."

"I'll get Flint," Amy said, not knowing what else to do.

"Claire!" Mrs. Whitely cried, her voice high.

"I'm OK, Mom," Claire said, getting up and walking slowly toward her.

Amy went to catch Flint. He was grazing nonchalantly on a patch of grass at the side of the ring. As Amy approached, he looked up at her, his muscles visibly tensing beneath his coat.

Amy pulled out a packet of mints from her pocket and held one out to him. "Here, boy," she said calmly.

She stood still and waited. Flint gazed at her for a moment longer, and then the lure of the mint became too strong for him. Stretching out his muzzle, he walked over to her.

"Good boy," Amy said, quietly taking hold of his reins.

As Flint crunched on the mint, he regarded her with his intelligent dark eyes.

Amy shook her head. "Now, Flint, that wasn't a nice thing to do." She patted his iron-gray shoulder. Flint might have a nasty streak, but she liked him. He was young and full of spirit.

She glanced over to the gate. Claire and her mom seemed to be arguing. "Looks like it's time to face the music," Amy said to Flint, her heart sinking. Clicking her tongue, she led him on.

"He has to go, Claire!" she heard Mrs. Whitely saying as she got near. "He's dangerous. Anyone can see that. Your father was a fool getting you a horse like that. I don't trust him."

"He's not dangerous, Mom!" Claire exclaimed. "He's just energetic."

"Energetic? He's going to break your neck!"

"No, he's not, Mom. He wouldn't do that!" Claire protested, turning to Amy for support. "Please tell her, Amy."

"He's just high-spirited," Amy said quickly. She saw the shock and concern on Mrs. Whitely's face and stepped forward, holding out her hand. "Hi, I'm Amy. I go to school with Claire."

"I told you about Amy, Mom," Claire put in. "She's the one who works at Heartland — the rescue center for horses."

Mrs. Whitely nodded distractedly. "Yes. Yes, I remember. Pleased to meet you, Amy." She looked back at Claire. "Oh, sweetheart," she said, shaking her head, "I just don't know what to do. I can't let you keep riding him if he's going to buck like that. What would you do if he threw you like that when no one was here?"

"But, Mom!" Claire protested.

"Maybe Claire could get some help with him," Amy broke in. "Have some lessons. He's really not dangerous, Mrs. Whitely. He's just taking advantage of her. Claire needs to learn to be firmer."

"I don't know," Mrs. Whitely sighed. She looked at Flint. "I guess I could ask Val Grant to work you into her schedule."

"No!" Claire interrupted. "I don't want to work with Val Grant. She'll make me hit him. I want Amy to help."

"I told you, I can't — not while he's here," Amy said. "Val Grant wouldn't allow it."

"Then we'll move him to Heartland," Claire said. "Won't we, Mom?"

Amy stared in surprise.

"Claire!" Mrs. Whitely exclaimed quickly. "You can't just make a decision like that."

"Why not?" Claire said. "I don't like it here. Val Grant is really hard on her horses. It's not at all like what I read about Heartland. Besides, Flint's really good with Amy. She can teach me what to do." She turned to Amy. "You will help, won't you?"

"Well, all our stalls are full at the moment," Amy said. She saw Claire's face fall. She desperately wanted to help, but there wasn't really room, and they were already so busy. "Well, it's still pretty warm," she said, thinking fast. "So I guess my pony, Sundance, could be turned out full-time. But only for a few weeks. Flint could have his stall."

Mrs. Whitely looked as if she didn't know what to say. "Well, that's very kind of you," she began, "but we've already paid this month's board."

"But, Mom," Claire begged her. "I'll do anything — just please say yes. Please let Flint go to Heartland."

Mrs. Whitely shrugged helplessly. "OK, then," she said at last. "If Amy thinks she can help, then I'll give him a second chance. But just for a month. If he hasn't improved, then he has to go, Claire."

"He'll get better," Claire said. "I just know he will!"

❧

When Amy got back to Heartland, she found Lou and her grandpa paying the bills in the kitchen. She told them about Flint. "He can have Sundance's stall," she explained. "Sundance can live out in the field for a while."

Grandpa nodded. "He'll love that, and it sounds like this friend of yours could use some help."

"When's the horse arriving?" Lou asked, opening the stable calendar so that she could schedule Flint's arrival.

"Mrs. Whitely said she'd try to rent a trailer for Saturday," Amy said.

"I could take ours over to get him," Grandpa said. "I don't have anything else planned."

"Great!" Amy said. "I'll call Claire's mom and let her know."

"Have you told Ty?" Lou asked.

"No. Do you know where he is?" Amy asked.

"In the feed room, I think," Lou said. "He'd been working on something for Dancer."

Amy hurried to the feed room. Ty was looking through one of Marion's books. She told him about Flint. "Her mom said she'll give him a month. If he's not improving in that time, she's going to sell him."

"Sounds like it's a case of the wrong horse with the wrong rider," Ty said. "They're just not a good fit."

Amy nodded. "Yeah, but Claire's desperate to keep him. And he's a fantastic horse. We've got to try to help.

If Claire can just learn to be firmer with him, then he'll start to respect her and stop taking advantage."

"It might take more than a month," Ty said, marking his place in the book before closing it.

"No, it won't," Amy said optimistically. "He's fine with me."

"But you've been around horses all your life," Ty said. "You just can't teach someone that kind of experience. It only comes with time."

Amy shrugged off his concerns. "It'll work out, you'll see." She changed the subject. "So where's Ben?"

"Guess," Ty said dryly.

"With Red?" Amy said, her heart sinking.

Ty nodded. "He's riding him up in the ring — for the second time. You know, he's probably only done about two hours' yard work today. If I ask him to do something, he does it. But if I don't, he just hangs around in the tack room or Red's stall. Half the time it's easier to do the job myself than to waste time tracking him down. I tried saying something, but it made no difference. "

"Do you want me to talk to him again?" Amy offered.

Ty shrugged. "We could get Lou to. He might listen to her."

"Let me try first," Amy said. Somehow involving Lou made it seem like an official complaint, and she was still hoping that Ben was just taking time to settle in.

"OK," Ty said in a reluctant tone. "Good luck."

As Amy walked up to the schooling ring, she wondered what she was going to say.

Ben was cantering Red around the ring. Along one side he had set up a line of fences. As Amy reached the gate, he turned Red toward them.

Amy frowned. Red's neck and shoulder were drenched with sweat. Seeing the jumps, Red threw his head high and plunged sideways to the left. Ben yanked on the reins and pulled Red into a tight circle, trying to get him to bend to the right.

Amy stopped and watched. Red was fighting Ben. He looked totally wound up.

Again, Ben made a small practice loop and turned Red toward the fences, and again Red plunged excitedly forward.

"No!" Ben shouted, pulling on Red's mouth and forcing him to back up several steps.

Amy flinched when she saw Red throw his head up as he fumbled backward.

Ben turned Red into a tight circle again, harsh thumps of his legs driving the horse forward. Amy knew that he was trying to stop Red from rushing too fast to the fences — but the firmer he got, the more excited Red became.

Amy forgot that she had come to talk to Ben about work. She ran to the gate. "Give him a break, Ben! Can't you see you're confusing him even more? He doesn't know what you want."

Ben pulled Red into a halt and swung around in the saddle. "What?" he demanded.

His eyes looked angry, but Amy refused to back down. "You're just frustrating him more by making him canter in small circles like that!" she exclaimed.

"He has to learn!" Ben said. "The show's in three weeks."

"He's not going to learn anything in that state," Amy protested. "Look, just take him out on the trails and let him cool off a bit. You can try again tomorrow."

Ben shook his head stubbornly. "I'm not giving in to him. He's going to learn *now*, or else this was all for nothing."

Red snorted and sidestepped. Shortening his reins again, Ben pushed him into a canter.

"Ben!" Amy exclaimed, feeling her temper rise.

But Ben took no notice. He cantered Red in a circle, ignoring Amy's protest. Other than throwing herself in front of the horse, there was nothing Amy could do except watch.

To her relief, however, she realized that the moment's halt at the gate had calmed Red down slightly. Instead of fighting Ben, he was now cantering smoothly, lowering his head, and softening his jaw.

Ben turned him into the line of jumps. Amy held her breath.

"Steady, boy!" she whispered as Red approached the fences with his ears pricked but in a much calmer state of mind. Ben let him go, his stride lengthened before the first fence, and they flew over all three with perfect pacing.

At the far end of the ring, Ben pulled him up. "Good boy!" he exclaimed, patting him hard.

He rode Red down the ring toward Amy. The stubborn angry look had vanished from his eyes.

"See!" he said triumphantly as he got close. "That was much better! *Now* I'll take him out for a trail ride. You should never give in to a horse, Amy," he said as she opened the gate for him. "They have to learn to do what you want, when you want. If they don't learn that, then you'll never have complete control."

With that, he rode Red out of the gate and headed toward the woods. "See you later."

Amy watched him go, not knowing how to argue her point and make Ben understand. Although he had succeeded with Red using his methods, there was no way she could agree with him. What was the point in having complete control if the horse didn't want to work for you? She truly believed a horse and rider were far more successful when they formed a partnership. And if that meant sometimes giving in to the horse or accepting that the horse was a living, breathing creature that was going to have off days just like humans, then so be it. As far as she was concerned, it was a small price to pay to have a horse that loved you and that would try, heart and soul, to please you.

She walked slowly down to the barn. Like a lot of competitive horse people, Ben clearly didn't share her beliefs. But then she didn't have to put up with seeing those other people riding their horses every day. It really bothered her watching a horse being trained in this manner at Heartland.

"Did you talk to him?" Ty asked, appearing from the tack room. "Is he going to cut down on his time with Red and put more into barn work?"

Amy suddenly remembered that she had gone to the training ring to talk to Ben about his contribution to Heartland. "I — I didn't get around to it," she admitted. "He's taken Red on the trails to cool him down."

"What?" Ty exclaimed. "That's all he's done all day! If he isn't riding Red, he's grooming him or cleaning his tack. There's still sweeping to do and the feeding, not to mention that he was supposed to exercise Jasmine today."

Amy saw the frustration in his eyes. "Look, don't worry, I'll talk to him when he gets back — I promise."

♍

Amy was sweeping up the loose straw around the muck heap when Ben rode back into the yard on Red.

He saw her and dismounted. "Working hard?" he said, patting Red.

Amy straightened up, feeling hot and annoyed. She pushed back the hair that stuck to her damp forehead. "Well, someone has to," she said shortly.

Ben looked at her in surprise. "What's up with you?"

"Ben!" burst out Amy, beginning to lose her temper with him. "You're supposed to be working as a stable hand here. You can't just ride Red all the time and leave all the work to me and Ty!"

"I don't!" Ben protested. "I helped Ty today. I mucked out six stalls and filled all the water buckets."

"Big deal!" Amy raised her voice. "What about the other twelve stalls and the grooming. What about working the horses!"

"Are you saying I'm not pulling my weight?" Ben said.
"Yes!"

"OK," he said shortly. "Then I won't ride Red at all in the day. I'll ride him after work."

"Good!" Amy exclaimed. "Maybe then we can get things done around here."

"Fine." Ben turned and marched across the yard with Red.

Ty came out of the back barn. "What was all that?" he said to her.

"Ben," Amy said. She saw Ty open his mouth to speak. "Don't even ask." She sighed. "I think I might have been too harsh. I better go say something to Lou, so she knows. I don't want her to find out another way."

She headed toward they house, telling herself to keep calm. Losing her temper wouldn't do any good. She had to keep reminding herself how Ben had come to be at Heartland in the first place, how they should be grateful to have the extra help — and the extra money.

Seeing Ben come out of Red's stall, she went over. "Look, Ben, I didn't mean to go off on you like that. It's just that we need you to help out more."

"Yeah. Fine," Ben said shortly.

Amy bit back the angry words that flew into her head. "Come on, Ben. I'm really sorry. I didn't mean to start a fight." But Ben didn't change his expression. Amy wondered if Ben was still upset with Red's behavior in the ring. Maybe that was what was on his mind. "You know, there are lots of supplements you could use to help calm Red down. Honey's good, and valerian. They're great for helping a horse's concentration. We could add some to his grain."

"Red doesn't need calming down," Ben said, shutting

the stall door with a bang. "He just needs to learn discipline."

"Discipline!" Amy exclaimed. "He was so dizzy he couldn't even see the fence!"

"He's my horse, and I'll decide how to train him," Ben said angrily.

"Even if you stress him out?" Amy shot back. "It's normal for young Thoroughbreds to be high-strung. I don't see why you don't want to try a supplement."

"No way — I'm not giving him any of that herbal crap," Ben said.

"Crap!" Amy gasped.

"Everyone knows that stuff doesn't work," Ben said. "Give what you want to the other horses here, but Red's sticking to his regular feed." He picked up his tack and turned to go and then hesitated. "Listen, Amy, what you do at Heartland is your business, but keep in mind that I never *asked* to come here and learn about it." With that, Ben marched off before Amy could respond.

OK, Amy thought, *that's it. I can't take any more of this.* She stormed up to the back barn to find Ty. She had *tried* being patient with Ben. She had tried giving him time. But she was not going to stand around and listen to him trash her mom's remedies and berate their work at Heartland.

"So how'd it go?" Ty asked casually. Then he looked at her expression. "OK — not good."

"You will *not believe* what Ben just said!" Amy exclaimed. The words tumbled out of her as she told Ty about her conversation with Ben.

"He said that?" Ty said.

"Yes!" Amy cried. "This is just so crazy! Why's he here? He doesn't believe in alternative remedies, I hate the way he treats his horse, and he hardly does any work!" Her eyes flashed. "Well, I've had enough! He's made it clear he has no real interest in being here. I'm going to talk to Lou."

"Well, what are you going to say?" Ty said.

"That we should get rid of him!" Amy said, with exasperation. "Right away!"

Chapter Six

Amy threw open the back door. Lou was busy updating the billing on her laptop. She looked around in surprise as Amy burst in.

"I need to talk to you," Amy said.

"What's up?" Lou asked, concerned. Just then the phone rang. "Hang on a sec," she said.

Amy sat down impatiently at the table. She wanted to get this sorted out right away. She knew the arrangement with Lisa was really convenient. Heartland needed the money and the help, but there was no escaping the fact that Ben just wasn't right for Heartland.

"Oh, hi, Lisa," Lou said into the phone. "Yes, this is Lou."

Amy turned around in surprise. "Lisa Stillman?" she mouthed at Lou.

Lou nodded at her.

Amy groaned inwardly. *What bad timing!*

"Yes, yes, Ben's settling in just fine," Lou said. Amy started to shake her head frantically but Lou had turned away and didn't see. "Yes, I'm sure," Amy heard her say. "No, there haven't been any problems. Why, did you get a different impression?"

There was a pause. Amy could just imagine what Lisa was saying. Amy wondered if Ben had told her anything. When Lou spoke her voice was serious.

"I understand," she said. "Yes . . . yes, I guess it is best that we know."

Amy felt surprised. What was going on?

There was another silence.

"I see," Lou said at last. "Oh, I'm sorry to hear that. Ben's been through a great deal."

Amy stared. What *was* Lisa saying?

"Well, like I said," Lou continued, "he seems to be doing just fine. But I'll let you know if there are any problems. Yes, of course, I won't say anything. You have my word. Thanks for calling, Lisa. Bye."

"What was that about?" Amy demanded as Lou hung up the phone.

Lou turned, a small frown creasing her forehead. "It's Ben."

"Yeah, I figured," Amy said impatiently.

Lou sat down slowly at the table. "Look — I'll tell you what she said, if you promise not to repeat it."

"OK," Amy replied, intrigued. "I promise."

"Lisa was checking in to see how Ben is doing," Lou explained. "She was worried he might have been a bit reluctant to take on some of the chores and really devote himself to working here. She said he's had a troubled background and he's had some problems adjusting in the past."

"Like what?" Amy asked, prepared to hear Lou out.

Lou sighed. "Well, his parents divorced when he was ten, and after that he started skipping school and basically got into a lot of trouble. Lisa said that because his mom wasn't coping very well with the divorce, she decided it was better if Ben didn't live with her. So she sent him to live with Lisa, thinking a new school and a fresh outlook might do him good. Lisa said it was a rough transition for Ben when he came to Fairfield. She thinks that, at first, Ben felt his mom was abandoning him, just as his dad had done. Then, after about a year or so, he got into riding. She said he was a natural, and once he started spending his time in the stables, he really loved being at Fairfield. The stable became his life."

Amy was stunned. "I had no idea about any of that."

"Lisa said she's a little worried that Ben now thinks that she's abandoning him — since she kind of volunteered him to come and work with us. That's why she was calling — to see how he was doing and make sure he's all right." Lou frowned. "But he's been fine, hasn't he?"

"Well . . ." Amy wondered what to say. "Actually," she admitted, "there have been some problems."

"But the other night you said everything was OK," Lou said quickly.

"No, I didn't," Amy said. "But I didn't get a chance to explain because Scott called. At first I thought it was just because Ben was new and he was getting used to Heartland. But things have gotten worse." She told Lou about her argument with Ben and how she had been coming to ask Lou to fire him.

"Oh, gosh," Lou said, when she'd finished, "that's not good." She looked at Amy quizzically. "And do you still feel the same?"

Amy hesitated. "I don't know," she said slowly. "I mean, I feel bad about all he's been through, but he pretty much said that he doesn't want to be here. Maybe he just wants to go back to Fairfield."

"Think of what Ben's been through, Amy," Lou said. "Lisa really thinks this is a good opportunity for him. That he'll feel more important at Fairfield after he's had a chance to learn and share all of Heartland's remedies. She thinks it's a good chance for Ben to feel like he belongs. After all that's happened to him, I don't want to take that chance away. I think he'll come around. We just need to be patient and give him some more time."

Amy thought about everything that Ben had said. "I'm not so sure he'll ever accept Heartland's ideas."

"Amy, we need to give him time to think about it," Lou persuaded.

"But why should we?" Amy demanded. "Worse things have happened to us, and we haven't gone around expecting people to give us special treatment. At least Ben's still got his mom — we don't!"

"No, we don't," Lou said quietly. "But what we do have is the knowledge that Mom loved us every minute of her life. Despite everything that happened, we've never had any reason to doubt that." She took Amy's hand. "Amy, you grew up here — at Heartland — with both Mom and Grandpa to love and care for you. Ben hasn't had that kind of stability." Lou shook her head. "Think about it. How would you have felt if Mom hadn't been as strong as she was and had sent you away after she and Dad separated?"

Amy was silent as Lou's words sank in. It was a thought too horrible to even contemplate.

Lou's voice softened. "Come on, Amy. Let's not turn our backs on Ben. This must be a difficult time for him, and, somehow, I can't help thinking that Heartland might be the best place for him right now." She squeezed Amy's hand. "Can't we at least try to help?"

Slowly, Amy nodded. "OK," she said. "If you really

think he's better off here, he can stay. I'll try to be more understanding."

Lou looked relieved. "Thanks, Amy, I really appreciate it. And you know, I think it might be best if we don't let him know that we know about his past," she added. "He might be upset with Lisa for telling us."

"I won't say a word to him," Amy agreed. "And I won't tell anyone — except Ty."

"No, Amy. You can't even tell Ty," Lou said hurriedly. "I promised Lisa that I wouldn't tell anyone. I'll explain the situation to Grandpa, but we have to keep it in the family."

"But I can't keep it from Ty!" Amy argued. "What will he think when I tell him that we're not going to fire Ben? This affects him, too. If Ben doesn't pull his weight more, and we don't put some kind of pressure on him, Ty is going to get suspicious."

"Just tell him I insisted that Ben was given a bit more time," Lou said. "Say that we owe that much to Lisa since she is paying us to train him in the first place. I don't mind if you blame it on me and the finances. But promise you won't tell him, Amy."

Amy looked at her reluctantly and sighed. "OK, I promise."

"Listen, Amy," Lou said gently, "things will work out — I'm sure of it. Ben just needs some time." She

smiled at her. "We help horses with problems all the time
at Heartland. Can't we help Ben as well?"

❧

Amy walked back to the yard, deep in thought. Ty
was filling a water bucket at the faucet. "How did it go?"
he said. "What did she say?"

"She wants to give Ben a second chance," Amy replied.

"You told her what he said about Heartland and not
even wanting to be here?" Ty said in surprise.

Amy nodded. "She still felt we should give him more
time."

Ty frowned. "Why aren't you mad at her?"

For once, Amy wished that Ty didn't know her so
well. "Well, maybe she's right. Ben might just need more
time to settle in."

She saw Ty look at her in astonishment.

"Anyway, we owe it to Lisa to try to make it work,"
she said quickly. "And as much as I'm not sure he'll ever
fit in, I guess we've got to respect that. And a little extra
help is better than none, right?"

Ty shrugged but didn't say anything.

"I'll go and talk to him again," Amy said. "Where is he?"

"Bringing Jake and Solo in from the field," Ty said.

Amy smiled weakly and then turned to go up to the
turnout paddocks. She felt awful not telling Ty the entire
truth.

She found Ben walking through the gate with the two horses. "Do you want a hand?" Amy said quietly, stepping forward to take Solo's lead rope.

"Thanks," Ben said.

Amy fidgeted with Solo's lead, not able to look Ben in the eye. *This is* so *awkward*, she thought. "Look . . ." she started.

"Amy . . ." Ben began at the same time.

They both stopped. "Go on," Ben said.

"I was just going to say that I'm sorry we argued before," Amy said.

"No, it's me who should be sorry," Ben said apologetically. "I overreacted. You guys have been good to have me here, and I just haven't been pulling my weight." He patted Jake. "I'll do a lot more from now on. Sometimes I just get so focused on Red that I lose track of everything else."

"OK," Amy said, surprised but pleased by his apology. "That would be good."

"I was frustrated with how things went with our ride today," Ben went on. "But I shouldn't have taken it out on you like that." The corners of his mouth flickered into a smile. "If one of the stable hands at my aunt's place had said those things, she'd have fired him."

Amy suddenly felt horribly guilty. Ben seemed genuinely sorry about what he'd said earlier. "Oh, we're not going to do that," she said lightly. "Come on."

They began to lead the horses toward the barn. "My mom called me today," Ben said. "She wants to come and watch me and Red at the show." He sounded casual, but Amy saw a tightness around his mouth. "I don't see her very often, you know."

"Oh, right. Why — why not?" Amy said uncomfortably.

Ben shrugged. "My parents got divorced when I was ten. Mom didn't deal with it very well and I was shipped out to live with Aunt Lisa when I was twelve. I guess Mom thought a break would do me good. It's been pretty permanent, though."

"Has she come to watch you at shows before?" Amy asked, trying to be positive.

"No," Ben said, and his voice was suddenly quiet. "If she makes it, this will be her first time."

"So you want to do your best then," Amy said, trying to sound sympathetic.

"I'd want that whether she was coming or not." Ben put his shoulders back. "I don't care what she thinks. Riding is about me and Red."

Amy glanced at him — for a moment he had shown her a much more vulnerable, likable side — but the barriers were back up again, and he had his old determined look back on his face.

As Amy put Solo away, she thought about what Ben had said. She didn't believe that he didn't care what his mother thought. She could tell that he cared deeply — maybe more than he wanted to. She wondered if that was why he had been so hard on Red in the ring earlier.

She was glad Lou had convinced her to let Ben stay. Things were pretty complicated for him. It seemed like the scars from his past were a long way from being healed.

For the next few days, when Amy was home from school, she noticed that Ben was making more of an effort to help around the yard, and he seemed more willing to stay late if necessary. However, it was clear that he was still not interested in learning about Heartland's real work. Although he pulled his weight, he didn't get involved in the healing side of things, and he didn't volunteer to work any of the problem horses.

On Saturday, Grandpa picked up Flint from Green Briar. When Amy saw the trailer coming back along the drive, she left the stall she was mucking out and came to meet him.

"How is he?" she asked, as Grandpa got out of the truck.

Jack Bartlett raised his eyebrows. "A bit of a handful. He just wouldn't let Claire lead him into the trailer. I had to do it in the end."

"Thanks, Grandpa," Amy said, feeling relieved that he had been there.

"Are you certain you're going to be able to help Claire with him, Amy?" Jack asked, looking concerned. "She's obviously very inexperienced with such a bold horse."

"I know, but I think I can help," Amy said, her gray eyes determined. "I really do."

Her grandpa looked at her for a moment and then smiled — a smile tinged with sadness. "Sometimes you remind me so much of your mom," he said quietly.

Amy met his eyes. So much of her time was taken up with just carrying on, but the loss and grief were always there, and it only took a time like this to bring her feelings flooding to the surface. For a moment the emotion threatened to overwhelm her, but just then Mrs. Whitely's car drew up and stopped beside the trailer.

Amy smiled at her grandfather and blinked hastily as Claire opened the door and jumped out.

"Wow!" Claire said, looking around at Heartland's barns and paddocks. "It looks just like in the magazine."

"I guess it does," Amy said, pushing her feelings back down and forcing her voice to sound light. She smiled at Claire. "I'm glad you like it."

There was a kicking sound from inside the trailer.

"We'd better let this horse out," Jack Bartlett said, beginning to unfasten the bolts on the ramp and the side door.

Glad to have something to do, Amy stepped into the

trailer. Claire followed her. Seeing Claire, Flint flattened his ears and snaked his head forward.

"Here, I'll take him," Amy said as Claire shrank back. She moved swiftly in beside Flint's neck and untied the lead rope. Flint shook his head, but she held on. "Easy now," she said, stroking him until he calmed down.

"OK!" she called to her grandpa outside.

Jack Bartlett lowered the ramp, and Amy backed Flint out.

Ty and Ben had come to see what was going on. "Nice horse," Ben said appreciatively as Flint snorted and looked around.

"Very," Ty agreed. "He looks like he's got a fair amount of spirit."

Claire stepped forward. With a squeal, Flint struck out with his front hoof.

"Be careful, Claire!" her mom gasped.

"He's just feeling unsettled," Amy said, uncomfortably aware of Mrs. Whitely's presence. "He's a little nervous. It's all new to him, that's all." She started to lead Flint around to try to calm him down.

"Can I get you some coffee?" Jack offered.

Amy was relieved to see Mrs. Whitely nod. If Flint was feeling wild, then the last thing she wanted was to have Mrs. Whitely watching. After all, they were trying to persuade her he was safe.

"So what do you think?" Amy said to Ty.

"He doesn't look naturally aggressive," Ty said.

"You must be joking!" Ben exclaimed. "You saw what he just did."

Ty looked at him impatiently. "You can tell by looking at his head he's not naturally aggressive. He looks intelligent, strong willed, and difficult, but not mean."

Amy smiled at him. She was glad to know that he saw the same traits in Flint's face that she did.

However, Ben looked less than impressed. "Yeah, and next you'll be telling me that you're checking his astrology sign as well!"

Amy tried to explain, hoping to gain his interest. "Ty's right," she said to him. "You *can* tell a horse's personality from its head. The shape of a horse's eyes, ears, muzzle, and lips all give you clues to what its personality's like."

Claire looked fascinated. "Really? So what does Flint's head say about him?"

Amy looked at the Thoroughbred. "Well, his large eyes and nostrils and slight moose nose suggest that he's intelligent and bold, but his long, flat chin, long mouth, and the way his ears are set close together also suggest that he might be strong willed and difficult. He looks like the sort of horse that needs to respect his rider."

"You can tell all that just from his face?" Claire said in astonishment.

Amy nodded.

"So what do I have to do to get him to stop him biting me?" Claire asked.

Amy hesitated. "You have to gain his respect. But it might not be easy."

"I don't care," Claire said. "I'm prepared to put in the hours and do whatever it takes to make it work. I just don't want to have to sell him."

"Well, we'll help you all we can," Amy said. "Won't we, Ty?"

"Sure," Ty said. He smiled at Claire. "If you're really determined to keep him, then there's no reason why things shouldn't work out."

"Well, I am," Claire said.

Just then, Mrs. Whitely came out of the house. "Are you coming home with me now, Claire?" she asked.

Claire looked uncertainly at Amy.

"I think it might be best just to let him get used to his new surroundings today," Amy said. "We'll start work tomorrow."

"OK," Claire said. "I'll see you tomorrow then." She glanced at her horse. "Bye, Flint."

The gelding stared into the distance and ignored her.

Claire looked at him for a moment longer and then hurried away.

"So," Amy said, beginning to walk Flint across the yard to the back barn, "do you think Claire will learn to handle him?"

"It's not going to be easy," Ty said seriously.

"That's for sure!" Ben said, joining in the conversation. "I'd say it'll be next to impossible! It's obvious a girl like that's never going to be able to handle a high-spirited Thoroughbred like Flint. I don't know why you're even bothering."

Ty swung around. He was obviously fed up with Ben's negative attitude. "No, Ben," he said. "I guess you wouldn't."

"What's that supposed to mean?" Ben demanded as Amy led Flint into the stall.

"How could you possibly understand why we want to help Claire? You're not remotely interested in how we work around here!" Ty snapped.

Amy came to Flint's door. "Ty . . ." she said, seeing the expression drop on Ben's face.

Ty ignored her. He seemed to have something he wanted to say. "Do you know what it's like to really want something, Ben?" he asked. "To want something so bad that you're prepared to fight for it? I'm guessing that you've had it easy all your life. So Claire's not as confident as you, but if she wants to fight to keep Flint, then we'll help her. Heartland's not just about helping horses, it's about helping people, too." He shook his head. "Not that you'd ever understand that." Glaring at Ben, he turned and walked away.

"What's up with him?" Ben exclaimed. "What did I do to deserve that?"

Amy let herself out of the stall, not knowing what to say. Ty hardly ever lost his temper. However, she was sure that Ben's comments about Claire had pushed Ty over the edge. The strain of putting in so many hours, now that they had a full yard, was obviously getting to Ty. And she understood how frustrating it had to be for him to have to deal with Ben, whose heart just obviously wasn't in it.

"He'll be OK," she said awkwardly. "He's just been working really hard lately and he's tired." She smiled at Ben. Trying to avoid further discussion, she changed the subject. "Look, how about we finish with the stalls and go out for a ride?"

After she had finished her share of the stalls she went to find Ty. She hadn't seen him since his outburst because she wanted to give him some time to cool off.

She found him lunging Moochie in the training ring. When he saw Amy standing at the gate, he brought the big bay hunter to a halt.

"Whoa, there," he said, gathering up the lunge line and leading the horse over to her.

"Hey," she said.

"Sorry about earlier," he said, glancing at the ground. "I really lost it back there. Who does Ben think he is? Telling us that we shouldn't bother with a horse and rider. That's what Heartland's all about." He shook his head. "He's really getting to me."

"I noticed," Amy said with a smile. She cleared her throat, wondering how Ty was going to take the news that she was just about to go on a trail ride with Ben. "I'm going out on the trails with him," she said. "We're going to take Solo and Gypsy." Ty just stared at her. "They could do with the exercise. Umm, you could come, too," she offered quickly.

"No thanks." Ty shook his head. "I don't get it, Amy. A few days ago you wanted to see him out of here as much as I did, so why are you now going out of your way to spend time with him?"

Amy avoided his gaze. "I just think he needs more time to get used to this place. I'm doing it for Lou. She thinks if we try he'll decide to get more involved." She looked up. "Come on, why don't you come? You could bring Moochie. It'll be fun."

"Wild horses couldn't drag me," Ty said with a faint smile, and turning Moochie away from the gate, he walked off.

Amy felt awful. She felt as if she had betrayed him. Sure, he'd made light of the situation, but she knew that, deep down, he must be feeling very confused and frustrated with her as well.

"See you later then," she said.

Ty nodded briefly in reply.

✷

Twenty minutes later, Amy and Ben were out on the trails and cantering along a wide grassy track. Amy glanced across at Ben. He was a very good rider, and he controlled headstrong Gypsy very well. A sixteen-hand, Dutch-bred mare, Gypsy had been sent to Heartland so they could cure her of her bucking habit. She was now almost ready to go home. Although she was still a spirited ride, she had stopped her frequent bucking rampages.

"Do you want to trot?" Amy called.

Ben nodded and eased the powerful black mare down into a trot. He patted her neck as she eased her pace.

Amy slowed Solo and brought him to a trot beside Gypsy. "She goes well for you," she said.

"She's a nice horse," Ben said. "What do her owners do with her in the show ring?"

"Mainly dressage," Amy said. "But I think they hope to do some eventing as well, now that she's stopped bucking. She's only five years old."

"What did you do to stop her bucking?" Ben asked curiously.

"We strapped a dummy on her back and let her buck as much as she wanted until she realized the dummy wouldn't come off no matter how hard she bucked. Once she realized that, she pretty much stopped. We changed her diet and used herbs and lavender oil to calm her down, and then we got on her ourselves. She was still pretty feisty at first, but she's doing well."

Ben smiled teasingly. "And I guess you analyzed her personality, too. That must have helped."

"It did, actually," Amy replied. "If you look at her head you can see that her forehead slopes back from above her eyes to her ears, and she's got a sloping muzzle and narrow nostrils. Those things suggest that she might be stubborn and willful. We've been working to encourage her to cooperate with people rather than resist them. We'll just need to have the owner come for some training sessions to learn how best to work with her personality."

Ben laughed. "You really believe all that stuff, don't you?"

"Yes," Amy said simply.

"OK," Ben challenged her. "So what's Red like?" He grinned. "Go on — analyze his personality."

Amy envisioned the big chestnut horse. "Well, he's got a wide forehead, a long mouth, and a flat, narrow chin, which suggest that he is very intelligent and probably a fast learner," she said thoughtfully. "His almond-shaped eyes and fluted nostrils also say that he's likely to be trusting and cooperative."

"Go on," Ben said.

Amy looked at Ben with a half smile and continued. "However, the slight dish in his face suggests that he is quite sensitive and needs to be handled carefully. He needs understanding. If you push him too hard he will lose confidence." Amy glanced at Ben. His forehead was furrowed in a slight frown. "Well? What do you think?" she asked. "You know him best. How'd I do?"

"It's actually not that far off," Ben admitted.

"See!" Amy said, triumphantly.

"Yeah, but you know him pretty well now," Ben said quickly. "How do I know that you can tell all that from his head and not just from seeing him in action?"

"You don't. You just have to trust me," Amy said. "It's like a lot of our work. It might not make exact sense, but we get the results." She looked at him. "And that's what matters."

"Maybe," Ben said. Then he patted Gypsy. "But I think I'll stick to science."

Despite his words, Amy thought that she sensed a slight change in his attitude.

They rode round a bend, and the trail widened out again. "Come on," she said, deciding not to persuade him anymore for now. "Let's canter!"

Chapter Seven

After lunch, Amy went to check on Flint to see how he was settling in. "I think I'll take him out in the training ring for twenty minutes or so," she said to Ty.

He nodded. "Do you have any idea how to help Claire?"

"Well, first I thought I'd get her to do some T-touch on him," Amy said. "Then she can start working him from the ground, lunging him to start, and then moving on to work him without the lunge line."

"That's a good idea," Ty said. "That should build the relationship between them."

Amy looked at Flint standing at the back of his stall. "He's not exactly what you'd call a friendly horse, is he?"

"Maybe there's something else behind his behavioral

106

problem," Ty said thoughtfully. "Do you know anything about his history?"

Amy shook her head. Normally she would have asked about the horse's history, but she hadn't taken on Flint in the usual way. "I'll ask Claire first thing tomorrow though," she said. She went into the stall. "Come on, Flint. Let's do some work."

Just as she had explained to Ty, she was planning to have Claire start working Flint from the ground, controlling him with a lunge line attached to his halter, and getting him to work through the gaits, change direction, back up, and come to the center when she told him to. The eventual aim was for Claire to be able to work Flint without a lunge line, just using voice commands. Amy was sure that this sort of work, called liberty work, would help Claire and Flint to develop a bond based on mutual trust and respect.

However, before Claire started, Amy wanted to find out whether Flint had ever been lunged before. She snapped the line onto his bridle, picked up the whip, and led Flint out of his stall.

Although at Heartland they never used whips to hit a horse, in liberty work the lunge whip was used as a guide for the horse — you could place it in front of him to slow him down, point it at his shoulder to keep him out at the side of the ring, or snap the whip on the sand to encourage the horse forward. Marion had always told Amy to think of a lunge whip not as a whip but as an extension of her arm.

Once in the circular training ring, Amy sent Flint out to the end of the lunge line. It quickly became obvious that he had been through this routine before. On command, he walked, trotted, and cantered circles around her.

After ten minutes, Amy decided to start teaching him some new commands, but she needed someone to help her out. She was about to go and ask Ty when she saw Ben with his pitchfork, standing by the muck heap. She thought that he was watching her. In fact he looked as if he might have been there for a while.

"Hey," she called over to him.

Ben raised his hand in greeting.

Amy made a snap decision. "Do you want to come help? I could use a hand."

Ben hesitated and then he nodded. "Sure," he called back.

When he reached her, Amy explained what she was going to do. "I need to teach him to change direction on command," she said. "Can you lead him on the outside and then encourage him around when I say 'turn'?"

"Sure," Ben replied with a shrug of his shoulders.

Amy clicked her tongue and told Flint to walk on. After a full circle, she said, "Turn."

Ben guided Flint around.

They repeated the exercise a few times. "So why are we doing this?" Ben asked.

"It's the first step toward liberty work," Amy said. "You teach the horse the commands on the lunge line, and when he's learned the commands you remove the lunge line to see if he will still obey you when he's free."

"But why?" Ben said.

"Because it helps develop the relationship between horse and rider," Amy explained.

Ben gradually started to move away from Flint's head until the horse was turning with no guidance apart from Amy's voice.

"That'll be enough for today," Amy said. She was pleased, both with the speed of Flint's learning and with how helpful Ben had been. He might say he didn't believe in alternative techniques, but when he dropped his skeptical act he seemed far more open-minded. He had seemed to sense exactly when Flint had needed his guidance and when to back away.

"Thanks," Amy said to him. "You were great."

Ben shrugged. "No problem."

As Amy led Flint back to his stall, Ty looked out from Dancer's stall. "How was he?" he asked.

"Great," Amy replied. "I got Ben to help, and we started teaching him to turn on command."

"You got *Ben* to help?" Ty echoed. "How'd you manage that?"

"Ty," Amy said in a pleading tone, leading Flint into his stall and undoing the bridle. "Will you please give Ben a chance? He was actually very good with Flint."

She came out of the stall. Ty was standing in the aisle, his arms crossed, a frown on his face. "I have given him a chance. I keep giving him chances, and he never changes around me," he said. "I'm starting to think he's not worth my time. But you — you are always giving him the benefit of the doubt, and that's not like you."

"Thanks a lot!" Amy said, trying to laugh it off.

But Ty continued to frown. "No, I mean it. Something's going on. You're spending all this time with him — taking his side. Why?"

"Lou asked me to, you know that," Amy said quickly.

Ty raised his eyebrows. "Yeah, and you always do what Lou says," he said sarcastically. "Come on, Amy. It's more than that. This is me you're talking to."

Amy so wanted to tell him the truth. How would Lou even know if she told him? But she knew she couldn't — not because of Lou, but because of Ben. "Well, you know I'm trying to get along better with Lou. And besides, I happen to think that she's right," she said. "She really wants it to work out with Ben. So I want to try. We have too much at stake in our relationship with Lisa Stillman. And he just showed that he is capable of learning — he just needs to be approached in the right way." She saw the skepticism in Ty's eyes, and her voice rose defensively. "Look, you say it's not like me to be so patient, Ty. Well, it's not like *you* to be so judgmental. Why can't you just give Ben a break?"

She saw the hurt flash across Ty's face. "Amy, those are all the same reasons you gave before. I'm not being judgmental — I'm being honest." Without saying another word he turned and started to walk off.

Amy couldn't handle lying to Ty. She had to offer some sort of explanation. "OK, OK," she said desperately. "You're right. There *is* something."

Ty swung round.

Amy caught herself. "But — but I can't tell you what it is."

Ty stared. "What do you mean, you can't tell me?"

Amy saw the disbelief in his eyes. She shook her head. "Lou made me promise," she whispered.

A shutter seemed to fall across Ty's face. "OK," he said coldly.

"I really want to tell you," Amy burst out. "You have to believe me. I just can't break my promise to Lou. It's really not that big a deal — I just can't say anything." She looked at him pleadingly. "Please try to understand."

Ty's eyes were filled with disappointment as he looked at her. "You know, Amy, I can't understand what's going on. I feel like I don't even understand you anymore." He held her in his gaze. "I've gotta get back to work."

Amy felt horrible. From the very beginning, when Ty had started working full-time at Heartland, her mom had always made a point of telling him everything about the business, and after she had died, he had been like one of the family — sharing their grief and fighting with them to keep Heartland going. But now that Amy was keeping something from him, she felt like she was deliberately cutting him out of the family he had become a part of.

She didn't want it to be that way. But she had given Lou her word, and Lou was firm that only the Flemings should know. Amy could see that if things could work out for Ben without too many people knowing about his personal life, it would be for the best in the long run. She felt sure that if Ty understood the situation, he'd feel the same way.

But there's no way he'll understand about Ben, she thought, *unless I tell him.*

That night, when Amy went into the house, she went up to her sister's bedroom. Lou was getting ready for her date with Scott.

"What's up?" she said, seeing Amy hovering at her bedroom door.

"Ty," Amy said, sighing. "Lou, I feel I've just *got* to tell him about Ben. He can't figure out why I'm siding with him, and he's really upset about it."

"I understand, Amy — I really do," Lou said gently. "But please, let's give Ben a bit more time. Ty'll come around once Ben adjusts to being with us." She stepped forward, her eyes sympathetic. "I'm really sorry to put you in this situation, but I want to honor my word to Lisa. She's trying to protect Ben. Grandpa agrees with me — it's the right thing to do."

Amy didn't say anything. She could see Lou's point of view. She knew that if she were in the same situation, she wouldn't want everyone to know about her past and talk about her problems behind her back.

"I'm sorry," Lou went on, "but I'd really appreciate it if you'd trust me on this one."

"It's . . . fine," Amy sighed, wishing it could be different.

Lou smiled. "Thanks, Amy. You know, I'm here for you if you need to talk more about it. You know that, don't you?"

Amy bit her lip as she nodded. "What time's Scott coming?" she asked.

"Any minute now," Lou said, glancing at her watch. "I'd better get a move on or I'll be late."

Suddenly, there was the sound of a car arriving outside. Amy looked out the window. "That's him!" she said, smiling at her sister.

Lou followed Amy down the stairs as she raced to open the door.

"Hi, Amy," Scott said, as he came into the kitchen. He caught sight of Lou. "Hey," he said, "you look great!"

"Thanks," Lou said, blushing. "So do you." She started looking around quickly. "I'll — I'll just get my coat."

"It's in the hall," Amy said, secretly enjoying the way her usually very composed sister seemed to be falling to pieces now that Scott was here. It was good to see Lou's more vulnerable side sometimes.

Lou reappeared from the hall with her coat, and Scott opened the door.

"Have a great time, kids," Amy teased.

"Don't worry, we will," Scott said, smiling at Lou.

Amy woke up in the early hours of Sunday morning to the sound of the front door shutting and a car driving off. Glancing at the luminous hands on her bedside clock, she saw that it was two o'clock. She smiled. Things must have gone well with Lou and Scott!

There was no sign of her sister when Amy got up. It was Ty's and Ben's day off, but as usual Ty came by to help. He was quiet as they measured out the feeds.

"I'll start with the stalls in the back barn," he said to her once the horses had been fed and watered. Hardly even waiting for her answer, he strode off.

Amy sighed. She hated keeping a secret from him, and now that he knew she was hiding something, things were worse. But she didn't know what to say to make things better between them.

After a while, Amy saw Lou come out of the house. She hurried over. "So how did it go?" she asked eagerly.

Despite still looking half asleep, Lou smiled. "It was really fun! We had so much to talk about. And he was so funny."

"So are you going out again?" Amy prompted.

"Maybe," Lou said coyly.

"When?"

Lou smiled. "Tonight."

"Oh, Lou! That's great!" Amy said, hugging her in delight. "Wait till I tell Matt and Soraya!"

"Really, Amy, stop being such a matchmaker," Lou said. "It's only our second date."

❧

Claire arrived later in the morning. Amy decided to take it one step at a time. "OK, come into the stall," Amy said, holding Flint by the halter. Claire walked in nervously. Flint put his ears back. "No!" Amy told him sharply. "It's OK, Claire. Just come up to him and pat him," she said kindly.

She made Flint stand still as Claire patted him.

"First, you're going to learn how to do the T-touch,"

Amy said. She showed Claire how to use the pads of her fingers to push Flint's skin lightly over his muscles in small circles and explained how the therapy worked.

"After you've finished one complete circle, slide your fingers to a new part of his neck and do another," Amy said. "And go slowly. The slower you go, the more he will relax."

Amy watched Flint's eyes carefully. He didn't look like he was particularly enjoying the treatment, but he wasn't objecting to Claire's touching him, either. After a minute or two, he seemed to relax slightly.

"Go all along his neck and down the top of his back to his hindquarters," Amy said.

After about ten minutes, she let go of Flint's halter. He stood quietly while Claire worked.

"I like doing this," Claire said, looking up.

"We use it on all the horses here," Amy said. "It's particularly good for the ones that are tense or oversensitive, and it really improves your relationship with a horse."

After a bit, they took Flint up to the ring. Amy lunged him first. He was excited at the beginning, but after he had cantered several circles and thrown in a couple of high-spirited bucks, he began to calm down and to listen to Amy's commands.

"OK, you can take over now, Claire," Amy said, bringing him to a halt.

"He still looks a bit wild," Claire said uneasily.

"He'll be fine," Amy replied. "Trust me."

Claire reluctantly came into the ring. Amy smiled at her reassuringly and handed her the lunge rope before moving to the gate.

"Walk on," Claire said hesitantly.

Flint didn't move.

"Walk on." Claire's voice shook, as she moved the whip toward him.

Flint stamped his hoof into the sand and put his ears back threateningly. Claire quickly withdrew the whip. "He's not moving," she said, looking helplessly at Amy.

"Sound like you mean it," Amy said, feeling slightly exasperated.

Claire tried again, but this time Flint moved toward her, his ears flat. Claire gasped and jabbed at him with the whip. Then the end of the whip wrapped loosely around her ankle. As she bent down to unravel it, she lost her balance and stumbled to the ground. "Amy," she cried.

Flint reared up in surprise.

"No!" Claire cried, covering her face with her hands.

Amy was already scrambling over the gate. She reached Flint just as he came to the ground. "Easy now!" she said, grabbing hold of his bridle.

Snorting loudly, the Thoroughbred stared warily at Claire.

"Are you OK?" Amy demanded.

Claire nodded. "I thought he was going to attack me!" she said, getting to her feet.

"It's OK. You just startled him," Amy said. "He wasn't trying to attack you, he was just reacting to your fall. It's OK." She looked at Flint's tense eyes. This was getting them nowhere. "How about you watch for a bit more, and I'll talk you through what I do?" she said to Claire, who nodded gratefully.

She worked Flint for twenty minutes and then looked toward the gate. She knew Claire needed to work with Flint, but she didn't want to lose ground with him — he was being really good for her. She didn't want to finish the training session on a bad note.

She asked the gray gelding to halt, and he stopped on a dime. "I think I'll bring him in now," she called to Claire.

"OK," Claire said, looking relieved that she wasn't going to have to work him again. But Amy still felt a little guilty.

Amy led Flint over to the gate. "So do you know anything about Flint's past?" she asked. "How he was with previous owners — stuff like that."

"Um, a bit," Claire replied. "I know he was bred by a woman who kept him until he was five. She trained and showed him. He's six now, and I think he's had two other owners besides me in the last year."

"So it sounds like he's been through a lot of changes recently," Amy said. "Maybe that explains some of his behavioral problems. With three different owners in a year, no wonder he's feeling unsettled."

"I hadn't thought about it like that," Claire said. "But I guess you're right. It was probably pretty hard on him." She smiled rather sadly. "I kind of know how he feels."

Amy looked at her curiously. "What do you mean?"

"Well, since Mom and Dad separated, Mom's always getting new jobs and we keep moving," Claire explained. "I'm always starting at new schools and have to make friends over again. Since the divorce, we haven't stayed anywhere more than a year."

"That can't be easy for you," Amy said sympathetically.

Claire shrugged. "It's OK." Her voice lifted. "Mom seems to really like it here, though — maybe she won't want to move again. And we're closer to where my dad lives so I can see him more often. I can't wait for him to get back and see Flint again."

"Well, now that we know what's going on with Flint, we can use some essential oils and flower remedies to help calm him down," Amy said. "As he gets calmer, he'll hopefully be more willing to form a new relationship with you. The T-touch will also help. And we have to get you working him from the ground."

"I hope it works," Claire said hopefully.

Amy smiled reassuringly at her. "I'm sure it will."

❧

Ben arrived at lunchtime. "I'll give you a hand with the rest of the chores when I'm done with Red," he said when Amy went over to say hi.

"But it's your day off," Amy said in surprise.

He shrugged. "I haven't got anything else to do."

"Well, thanks then," Amy said, smiling at him. She was happy that he was making more of an effort.

"Mom called again last night," Ben told her as they walked to the tack room together. "I thought she might be calling to cancel, like she's done before, but she said she's definitely going to come." He picked up his grooming kit. "So I'd better get moving. Red and I have some work to do."

Amy started gathering a bunch of brushes that needed to be cleaned. After a bit, Ben led Red up to the training ring. She was just filling a bucket with bleach and water when Ty came marching up to the faucet.

"That's it!" he exclaimed, his eyes dark and angry. "I've had enough. I just can't believe that guy anymore!"

Amy didn't think she had ever seen Ty look so furious. "What is it?" she said, alarmed.

"Just come and see what he's doing to Red!" Ty exclaimed.

He stormed off toward the training ring.

Amy ran after him. "Ty! Wait!" But Ty didn't stop.

She hurried up to the ring to find Ben cantering an exhausted-looking Red in small circles, right in front of a jump.

"What does he think he's doing?" Ty demanded as Red fought for his head, his mouth foaming with saliva and his sides stained with sweat. "Could he be any harder on that horse? I can't stand by and watch this."

Amy took a deep breath and tried to rationalize the situation. She *hated* her new role as diplomat! "He's just trying to stop Red from rushing his fences," she said quickly. "Listen — this show he's going to in a few weeks is really important to him." Like Ty, she hated seeing Ben ride Red into the ground and she wished he would stop, but she was trying hard to understand him — to accept that he wasn't going to change his riding style overnight.

Ty turned on her. "So you actually approve of what he's doing?" he said incredulously.

"Of course I don't," Amy said. "But what can we do? Red is Ben's horse."

"But he's riding him on Heartland property," Ty said. His mouth hardened. "Well, if you won't say anything, Amy — I will."

"Wait, Ty!" Amy pleaded as she grabbed his arm to hold him back.

But it was too late. Ty shook her arm loose and headed straight to the fence. "What do you think you're doing, Ben?" he exclaimed.

Ben pulled Red to a halt. "What?" he said in surprise.

"Riding Red like that — look at him!" Ty pointed to the sweat foaming on Red's neck. "What are you going to accomplish by spinning the horse in circles?"

Ben's eyes grew colder. "Can't you see he's rushing at the jumps?"

"Oh, right, and you think what you're doing is going to stop him?" Ty demanded.

"Like you know anything about it!" Ben snapped.

"I know that if you get a horse upset like that it can't even think, let alone learn," Ty snapped back. "It's the stupidest thing I've ever seen."

"Well, thanks for your opinion," Ben said, digging his heels into Red's sides so that the horse broke into a canter again. "But I don't need your help."

Amy didn't want the situation to get out of hand. She rushed into the ring. "Ty, look — just let it go," she said.

He swung around. "Let it go?" he questioned. For a moment, Amy thought he was going to grab her shoulders and shake her, but then he seemed to stop himself. "You've never let something like this go in your life. You're always the first to speak out when a horse is mistreated. When did you let it all go?"

"But Ben's not mistreating Red — at least he's not being outright cruel," Amy argued desperately.

Ty looked to the top of the ring where Red was still making tight circles, his head bent, his neck foaming with sweat. "So you think *that's* not mistreating a horse?" he said, turning so that his eyes bored into hers. "It's one step from abuse."

Amy didn't say anything. She couldn't. She knew he was right.

Ty's eyes held hers for a moment, and then, shaking his head in angry disbelief, he pushed past her and walked away.

Chapter Eight

For the rest of the day, Amy felt that Ty was avoiding her. Instead of hanging around to talk like he usually did, he left right after the horses had been fed.

"He was in a weird mood all day," Ben commented, joining her as she watched Ty's car bump away down the drive.

Amy shrugged. There was no way she was getting into this conversation with him. "Oh, I guess. He's probably just in a bad mood."

"If you ask me, he's always in a bad mood," Ben said. "Doesn't he *ever* lighten up?"

"You don't know him," Amy said defensively. "He's OK. He's more than OK."

"Yeah, if you're an astrologically challenged horse," Ben said.

Amy glared at him and walked away.

"Hey, Amy! I'm sorry," Ben said, going after her.

She stopped.

"Look, don't get me wrong," Ben sighed. "I know you and Ty get along really well and that he's great with the horses you have here, but I wish he'd stop trying to tell me what to do with my horse."

"He only said those things because he cares about Red," Amy said.

"Are you saying I don't?" Ben demanded

"Well . . . not in the same way . . ." Amy began.

"Amy, Red is *the* most important thing in my life," Ben interrupted her. "I would never do anything to hurt him in any way."

"What about this afternoon? What about when things don't go your way?"

"Look — you and Ty might not agree with my methods," Ben went on. "But they're *my* methods, and I'm using them with *my* horse, and if either of you don't like that, then that's your problem, not mine. I'm not the only person who uses these kinds of techniques, you know."

Amy took a deep breath. Part of her wanted to yell at him to stop being so stubborn, to listen to Ty — to listen to her. But she knew it wouldn't do any good. She couldn't force him to change how he trained. That would only turn him against her, as well as against Ty. All she could do was be patient, give him time, and try to win him over.

⍺

The atmosphere in the yard did not improve over the next few days. Ty avoided Ben as much as possible and was painfully reserved with Amy whenever she was around. To take her mind off Ty, Amy threw herself into working Flint.

Claire came to Heartland every night after school. She was getting increasingly confident using the T-touch circles and massaging him with diluted oil, a remedy that Amy hoped would help settle him down. In the stall, at least, Flint seemed to be accepting Claire more and more. But as soon as he was out in the training ring, everything changed.

Claire seemed to lose all confidence once Flint was in an open space. She always ended up giving the lunge line to Amy and going to watch from the gate.

Amy told herself that it didn't matter. They were just taking things slowly, and it was better that Flint was at least learning the voice exercises with someone. She also had to admit that she loved working Flint. His intelligence meant that although he was a challenge, he was also a very quick learner. Amy was pleased to sense a bond growing between them.

On Friday afternoon as she walked up to his stall after

school, she noticed how relaxed he was. He was looking out over his stall door. He whinnied softly when he saw her.

Amy was delighted. It was one of the first signs of affection that Flint had shown. She hurried forward, digging a packet of mints out of her pocket. "Hi, boy."

He pushed his dark gray muzzle softly against her arm as she took a mint from the packet.

Just then, Ty came out of Dancer's stall.

"He's getting friendlier," he said, looking at Flint nuzzling Amy.

She nodded. "Did you hear him whinny?"

"Yeah."

Amy glanced up. Ty was watching her. "What?" she said, seeing concern in his eyes.

"He's supposed to be forming a bond with Claire, Amy, not with you."

"I know," Amy said quickly.

"So why are you the one who's working him?" Ty said.

"Well, Claire doesn't want to," she said defensively. "And anyway I'm not doing the hands-on work in the stall, Claire's doing it all now." She saw that Ty's eyes were still looking concerned. "Claire just needs more time to become confident!"

"She'll never gain confidence while you do everything for her," Ty said.

"But if she starts doing the ground exercises now, Flint could get worse," Amy protested. "I just want him to keep improving!"

"You're supposed to be thinking about Claire, too," Ty said. "She needs to improve, too. Or have you forgotten that? She'll never be comfortable with him if she feels like she's competing with you."

Amy felt the rush of color flood her cheeks. Deep down, she knew he was right, but she didn't want him to be. "I'm the one who's supposed to be treating him!" she said, her embarrassment giving her a defensive tone. "And I'll make the decisions!"

Ty stared at her. "*You'll* make the decisions?" He stared at her. "Since when do you make all the decisions? We used to treat the horses *together*. Or does my opinion not matter around here anymore?"

Amy swallowed, the color in her cheeks deepening as she realized what she had said. "I — I didn't mean it that way." She felt horribly uncomfortable. She had never spoken to Ty in such a way before. Since her mom had died, they had really relied on each other and decided on the treatment of the horses together.

Just then, Claire appeared at the top of the aisle. "Hi!" she called out, oblivious to the tension in the air. She hurried toward them. "How are you, Ty?"

"Fine," he replied, stepping back from Amy. He

smiled briefly at Claire. Amy had noticed that he always seemed to make a special effort to be friendly toward her.

"I've got a favor to ask," Claire said, looking at them both.

"Ask away," Ty said.

"Well, when we brought Flint here, I was in such a rush to get away that I left three of his blankets at Green Briar." Claire looked a little awkward. "I don't want to go there on my own in case I run into Val or Ashley. I was hoping that —"

"That one of us would come with you?" Ty finished for her.

Claire nodded. "Would you?" she said hopefully.

"Sure," Ty said with a shrug. "We can go in my car."

"Yeah, I'll come, too," Amy said. She smiled at Claire, trying to forget the argument with Ty. "We'll protect you from Ashley."

They got into Ty's car. Still oblivious to the tension crackling between him and Amy, Claire chatted away. Now that she had gotten over being shy, she was a lot of fun to be with.

When they reached Green Briar, there was no sign of the Grants. "I'll go with Claire to get the blankets," Amy said to Ty. "We'll be right back."

Ty nodded. "I'll wait here."

Amy and Claire found Flint's rugs.

"At least we haven't seen anyone," Claire said as they hurried back down the main stable aisle.

"I'm afraid you spoke too soon," Amy whispered. As they turned the corner toward the car, she had seen Ashley leaning against it, talking to Ty.

Claire stopped dead. "Oh, no."

"Come on," Amy urged. "Just stand up to her."

Ashley's back was turned to them. As they got nearer, they saw her flip her hair back and laugh and then lean closer to Ty.

Amy felt a surge of anger. She gritted her teeth and marched toward them.

"We could really use someone with your skills at Green Briar, Ty," she heard Ashley say. On the word *skills*, Ashley's voice dropped huskily. "You know, my mom would do anything to get you to work here."

"Ty's already got a job, Ashley!" Amy said.

Ashley turned. "Hi there, Amy," she said coolly. "Ty and I were just —" she glanced back at Ty with raised eyebrows — "chatting."

"Yeah, I heard!" Amy said angrily. "Well, Ty's not leaving Heartland. Are you, Ty?"

Ty gave a small shake of his head but glared at Amy. When she saw his face, she flinched. She couldn't believe she answered for Ty like that. She had just said exactly what she wanted to believe — that Ty would never leave Heartland. Things had been so difficult lately, she couldn't help thinking that Ty might actually be tempted by the Green Briar offer. And if he was, she hadn't done much to convince him to stay.

"That's too bad," Ashley went on, looking at Ty through her long eyelashes. "We could have a lot of fun. Still," she said, "it's not too late to change your mind. The position's still open. In fact, I bet you could name your price."

Amy threw the rugs on the backseat of the car. "Come on! Let's go!" She felt so mad at Ashley that she almost could have hit her. How dare Ashley try to talk Ty into going to Green Briar right in front of her! Seeing Ashley smile at Ty again, she almost exploded. "Come on, let's go!" she repeated, flinging herself into the front seat. She realized she was being rude and bossy, but the situation was almost making her ill.

"See you," Ty said to Ashley.

Amy slammed the door.

Claire hastily got into the backseat on Amy's side. "Too scared to come without reinforcements?" Ashley said to her under her breath, a sneer in her voice. "Get a backbone, Claire."

Claire looked away.

"Bye, Ty," Ashley called as Ty started the engine. "And don't forget about us."

✌

Amy was so frustrated that she didn't say a word all the way back to Heartland. Her stomach was in knots she was so upset. Once they arrived, she went straight to the feed room and tried to release her anger by making up the evening hay nets.

Claire came to find her. "Flint's ready," she said.

"OK," Amy said. She was hot from shaking up the hay and stuffing it furiously into the nets, but she felt slightly calmer.

"Ashley really got to you, didn't she?" Claire said tentatively as they walked down to the tack room together to get Flint's bridle and the lunging equipment. "Was it the way she was coming on to Ty?"

"Don't even mention Ashley to me," Amy muttered angrily. "She's not worth it."

"Oh — OK," Claire said. There was a pause. "So what are you going to do with Flint tonight?"

"Well, I'll work him on voltés — they're small circles," Amy said. "And then I think you should have a go and put him through the paces."

Claire looked panic-stricken. "Are you sure he's ready for me? I mean, he's being so good for you."

"Yeah, but he needs to be good for you," Amy said, remembering what Ty had said. "He's been a lot better with you in the stall. If you're firm with him, I think you'll find he'll be good outside as well."

Claire didn't look convinced.

Amy worked Flint for five minutes and then decided that it was time to hand him over to Claire. She halted Flint and called Claire into the middle.

"Are you sure?" Claire said nervously.

Amy nodded. "You'll be fine."

Claire walked cautiously into the center of the ring.

"Just stand beside me as I lunge him," Amy said. She sent Flint forward at a trot again and after three circles gave Claire the lunge rein. "OK, now you take over."

"No," Claire said quickly, trying to hand the line back.

"Go on," Amy said, refusing to take it. "It's OK. You need to do this, Claire."

But sensing Amy's lack of concentration, Flint slowed down and looked toward the middle of the ring. "Tell him to trot on," Amy said quickly to Claire.

"Trot on!" Claire said nervously.

Flint slowed to a walk.

"Go on — make him do it," Amy said more firmly.

But Claire shook her head and gave the lunge line back to Amy. "You do it. He'll do it for you."

With a sigh, Amy took the line back.

"Amy!" She looked out toward the gate and saw Ty. She wondered how long he had been watching.

"What?" she called.

"I need to talk to you a minute."

Amy brought Flint to a halt. "Can't it wait?"

"No," Ty said. "Not really."

Amy called Flint to her. The gray horse walked over obediently. Amy turned him to bring him in, wondering what it was that Ty needed to talk about so urgently.

"Claire can hold him for you, right, Claire?" Ty said.

Claire looked startled. "Well — er —"

"We won't be long," Ty said, smiling at her. "Just walk him around. Do some T-touch with him."

"OK," Claire agreed.

Amy walked over to the gate. "Yeah?"

"Let's not talk here," Ty said. "Come down toward the barn."

Amy followed him away from the gate. "So what's going on? Is everything OK?" she demanded.

"It will be," Ty said. "But only if you give Claire a real chance to bond with Flint. You have to let her work him on her own."

Amy stared at him. "What do you think I was trying to do? I forced her to take the lunge rope from me, but she made me take it back."

"You shouldn't have taken it." Ty shook his head. "I know you're only tying to help, Amy. But can't you see? While you're there, Claire doesn't stand a chance. Flint will turn to you for direction, and Claire will back down every time."

"So what do you expect me to do?" Amy said.

"Have some faith in her," Ty said. "Give her another chance."

Amy shook her head. "I have to think of Flint. His progress is too important. The horse has to come first. The horse always comes first."

Ty looked at her. "What about with Ben and Red?"

Amy looked defiantly at Ty. "That's not fair! You know it's not."

"Why not?" Ty said.

"I don't like the way Ben treats Red any more than you do," she cried angrily, "but there's nothing we can do about it. Not now, anyway. Look, if you're so willing to stand up for Claire, why aren't you more understanding about Ben?"

Ty laughed scornfully. "What's there to understand? He's a rich kid who cares more about winning than he does about his horse."

"That is *not* true!" Amy said. "Ben does care about Red — he cares a lot."

"Well, he's got a strange way of showing it!" Ty snapped. He shook his head. "I can't stand the way he treats Red. I know it takes a lot to train a jumper, but I think he pushes the limits. And it's hard to deal with something like that happening at Heartland. Look, I came here to work with your mom and follow her ideals, and I just don't think she'd be happy with what's going on." Just then, the phone started to ring in the house. "I'll get it," he said, and he walked swiftly away.

Feeling overwhelmed, Amy hurried back to the ring. Right now, she felt like she was being pressured from all sides, and it was all beginning to get to her. Everyone wanted something different from her, and she couldn't cope with it anymore. Then, as she turned the corner, she stopped dead. Claire was standing in the middle of the ring, and Flint was facing her.

"Go on, Flint. Away!" Amy heard her say. Flint hesitated, and Claire flicked the ground with the whip. "Go on!"

Amy held her breath, watching Flint's reaction.

Slowly, Flint walked to the outside of the ring.

Amy took a step back. She didn't want Claire to see her and be distracted. Amy wondered if she was actually going to try to lunge him.

Then she saw Claire tap the lunge whip on the ground. "And trot!"

Flint looked at her. "Trot on!" Claire said, using the whip on the ground again.

To Amy's surprise, Flint began to trot. She saw a flash of joy cross Claire's face. "And walk!" she told him, pointing the whip toward the front of his shoulder as Amy normally did. Flint slowed to a walk.

"Good boy!" Claire praised. "And turn!"

Claire almost tripped over the lunge line as Flint did

as she said. "And trot on!" she called. An amazed smile lit up her face as Flint broke into a trot again.

Amy felt a surge of delight, but she stopped herself from running up to the gate to yell congratulations. She didn't want to disturb Claire when she was doing so well.

After a few more minutes, Claire brought Flint to a halt again and then called him to the middle. He walked toward her.

"Good boy!" she cried, stepping forward to pat him.

Flint rambunctiously threw his head in the air, and Amy's heart stopped for a moment as she anticipated Claire shrinking back and letting Flint get away with it. But Claire had newfound confidence, and she stood her ground.

"No!" Amy heard her say firmly. Taking up the slack on the rope, Claire stepped closer and patted the gray's neck again.

This time Flint accepted her affection. He let out a snort, and then, bringing his head around, he looked at her.

Claire rubbed his forehead and smiled.

A wave of relief and delight overwhelmed Amy. She knew it was just the first step for Claire and Flint, but they were on their way to building a new relationship. And really, they owed it all to Ty. He had known that they were ready. Amy suddenly wanted to find Ty and tell him. Suddenly, all the arguments of the past ten days faded. She knew that their disagreements didn't really matter because they shared the same vision of what was most important.

She could hardly wait to share the good news with him. She looked in the feed and tack rooms and then remembered the phone ringing and wondered if he was still on the phone. The kitchen door was open. She ran toward the house. As she got near, she heard his voice carrying on a one-sided conversation. She slowed down, not wanting to disturb him.

"Yeah, the salary is extremely generous," she heard him saying. "And two days off a week sounds great."

Salary? Amy stopped. *Days off?*

There was a pause.

"Yeah, of course, I'll let you know, Mrs. Grant," she heard Ty say.

Mrs. Grant! Amy froze. Ty was talking to Val Grant about salaries and days off. And he was saying he'd let her know. Was he really considering taking the job at Green Briar?

She backed away from the house, then turned and ran across the yard and into the feed room. She sat down on a bale of hay, her stomach churning. Ty couldn't leave. How could she run Heartland without him? She buried her head in her hands and tried to fight back the tears.

A few minutes later, she heard footsteps coming up to the barn. Wiping the arm of her sweatshirt across her face, she jumped to her feet.

Ty entered. He stopped when he saw her. "What are you doing in here?" He frowned. "What's up?"

"Nothing," she said quickly.

"Are you OK?" he said, stepping closer.

"Yeah." Amy looked down as she felt the tears rise in her throat again.

"Amy?" Ty took hold of her arm. "What's wrong?"

"Nothing's wrong!" Amy cried, hurt and betrayal flooding through her as she looked at his concerned face. How could he look at her like that when he was planning on leaving? She knew things hadn't been easy for him since Ben had arrived, but she didn't think things were that bad. Even though she hadn't been completely open with him, she at least would have expected him to tell her if he really wanted to leave. She felt that it was all her fault. If she had been honest with him, things would never have gone so far. But there wasn't anything she could do, and it was probably too late to change his mind.

"Is there anything I can do?" Ty asked.

Suddenly, something snapped inside her. She wrenched her arm away. "No," she said. "This is something I have to deal with on my own. You can't do anything."

Ty's face paled, as if he took her words to mean much more than she intended. "Well, OK," he said, and walked out of the barn.

Amy collapsed onto the hay bale again and this time completely gave way to her tears. She couldn't face the thought of Ty leaving. She couldn't even talk to him about it.

Chapter Nine

Ten minutes went by before Amy had enough control of herself to go up to the training ring. She splashed some water on her face from Flint's water bucket and then went to see how Claire was coping. She had a responsibility. Mrs. Whitely trusted her with Claire and Flint's well-being. Amy took several deep breaths and hoped everything would be OK.

She found Claire lunging Flint again. He was cantering around her. Seeing Amy, she brought him to a halt. "Look!" she said in delight. "He's letting me lunge him!"

"That's great," Amy said, going into the ring.

Claire frowned. "Are you OK? You look — odd."

Amy managed a faint smile. "I'm OK, thanks."

"Ty was looking for you."

"Yeah, he found me. He just wanted to talk about one

of the horses," Amy lied. She patted Flint. "It really is great that you got him to lunge on your own."

"I know!" Claire said, caught up in her own delight. "I walked him around for a while and then did some T-touch. He was being good so I thought I'd just try lunging him, and he was fine. He was great!" She grinned. "I can't wait to tell Mom."

When Claire told Ty about her success with Flint back in the barn, he congratulated her warmly. "I knew you could do it!" he said.

"Thanks," Claire said, smiling at him. "I know I'm going to have to keep at it to build a really good relationship with him, but at least it's a start."

"That's great," Ty said.

After Claire had gone, Ty hardly said a single word to Amy until he left that evening. "I'm taking my day off tomorrow," he said curtly as he got his coat from the tack room. "So I'll see you Sunday."

Amy nodded. "Bye."

She watched Ty walk away, thoughts tumbling through her mind in a confused mess. Part of her wanted to run after him, to beg him not to leave Heartland, to tell him that she couldn't run the place without him. But there was another part of her that felt desperately hurt and utterly resentful that he would consider betraying her by going to Green Briar.

She swallowed. What was she going to do?

❧

The next morning, Claire arrived at nine o'clock. Amy had never seen her at Heartland so early before. "I can't wait to try lunging him again," she said. "Mom's not picking me up me till this afternoon. I thought maybe I could lunge him twice."

"Sure, as long as you keep both sessions short," Amy said. "So he stays focused."

"I could do some T-touch on him in between," Claire said. "And maybe let him graze a little."

Claire's first lunging session with Flint went well, and the second went even better. Amy watched from the gate. "You're doing great! He's really listening," she said encouragingly.

Just then, Ben joined her. "She has gotten better, hasn't she?" he said.

Amy nodded. "It's all about confidence," she said as Claire made Flint turn and canter in the opposite direction. "Now that she knows she can make Flint do what she wants, her confidence is really growing. Hey, Claire!" she called. "How about trying him without the lunge line?"

Claire brought Flint to a halt. "What? Really?"

"Yeah," Amy said. "Just use the whip as you've been doing," Amy said. "It's the same signals, just without the line. Let's see what he does."

Claire led Flint over to the gate, unsnapped the lunge line, and handed it to Amy. "Here goes."

She led Flint back to the center and then let go of his bridle. "Away," she told him. Flint obediently walked away, and then suddenly he seemed to realize that the lunge line was missing. He stopped.

"Use the whip!" Amy said quickly.

Claire tapped the whip on the floor. "Walk on."

Flint hesitated. Amy held her breath, but then to her relief the gray horse moved on.

"And trot!" Claire said quickly, tapping the whip on the floor again.

With no line attaching him to her, Flint broke into a trot. He trotted easily around the circle.

"And turn!" Claire called.

Spinning quickly on his haunches, Flint changed direction.

"That's amazing!" Ben said to Amy.

"Good job!" Amy shouted.

After a few more circuits, Claire brought Flint to a halt and called him to her. "That's a good boy!" she said, patting him in delight. "I'll do some more tomorrow. But I'd like to stop for the day. Wasn't he fabulous?"

"You both were!" Amy said, opening the gate as Claire led Flint over.

"I didn't think I could do it," Claire said, looking totally astonished. Her eyes shone. "Did you see the way he changed direction? He was so quick!"

Amy nodded. She had, and more important than that, she had seen the respect and trust in Flint's eyes as he had reacted to Claire's commands.

"He's like a different horse," Ben said to her as they followed Claire and Flint down the yard. "I mean, a week ago he wouldn't let her near him."

"And now he's willingly responding to her direction," Amy agreed. "Not because he's forced to, but because he wants to. And the stronger the bond between them gets, the harder he will try for her." She looked at him. "When they start to show, they'll have a real partnership. And he'll really try his hardest for her. What more could a rider want?"

Hoping her words would sink in, she walked away. The last thing Amy wanted was to sound preachy, but the only way things were going to work out at Heartland was if she could get Ben to start seeing things more like she and Ty did. She didn't want to have to ask Ben to go, but most of all she hoped that he would eventually want to stay.

Before Claire left that afternoon, she asked Amy whether she could ask her mom to come see Flint work the next day.

"Sure," Amy said.

"I think she'll be really impressed," Claire said happily. "OK, see you tomorrow then!"

"Yeah, see you," Amy replied.

She thought about what the next day would bring. How would she react to Ty? Would he tell her that he was leaving? In a way, she felt like she should tell him that she had heard him talking to Val Grant. But how would she bring it up? She couldn't tell him that she had listened to his private conversation, and if she did and he said that he was leaving, what was the point?

❧

Amy was mucking out a stall when Claire and her mom arrived on Sunday morning.

"Hello, Amy," Mrs. Whitely said. "Claire said it was OK if I came to watch today."

Amy nodded. "Sure."

"I'll go and groom Flint. Then can I take him to the ring?" Claire asked eagerly.

"Yes, but you might want to do some T-touch on him first," Amy said.

"OK," Claire said. She turned to her mom. "Come on,

Mom. I'll show you what T-touch is." Her eyes lit up.
"You could even do some!"

Amy looked at Claire in surprise. She had never seen
her look so happy and enthusiastic. The success of the
day before really seemed to have changed her. *I just hope
that Flint's as good with her today,* Amy thought. *It would be
awful if he acts up with Mrs. Whitely here.*

Five minutes later, Ben arrived, even though it was his
day off. He came to find her. "I'm going to take Red out
for a ride," he said. "Do you want to come?"

"Thanks, but I'd better not. Mrs. Whitely is here to
see Claire work Flint." Amy said. She put her pitchfork
down. "I hope he's good."

Ben nodded. "I'm sure he will be. See you later then."

Amy finished the stall and decided to go see how
Claire was doing. As she walked up the yard, she saw
Ben heading off toward the trails on Red.

"Have a good ride," she called.

Claire was working T-touch circles on Red's forehead.
Flint's neck was low and relaxed and his eyes half
closed. Amy felt relieved.

Mrs. Whitely smiled when she saw Amy. "Claire's
been explaining this T-touch to me. It's fascinating."

Claire looked around. "Do you think he's ready for
the ring now?"

Amy nodded. "Start off on the lunge rope, and then
when he's settled you can let him off."

Claire set off to the tack room.

Mrs. Whitely watched her go. "I can't believe the change in Claire," she said to Amy. "She's been so happy these last few days. She's hardly stopped talking for a moment!"

Amy nodded. "I think it's really helped her confidence to be able to get Flint to do what she wants."

"So she really is OK to handle him on her own?" Mrs. Whitely asked. "When she said I could come and watch her today, I have to admit I had my doubts. This improvement seems to have happened so fast."

"We've been treating him with some violet leaf oil to help calm him down, and the T-touch Claire's been doing has helped develop a bond between them," Amy explained. "But the real breakthrough came when Claire worked him on her own yesterday." She saw that Mrs. Whitely was intent to hear more. "I think she suddenly realized that if she was firm, he would do what she wanted. So she stopped feeling so scared of him," Amy went on. "Flint has started to respect her, and now, hopefully, their relationship can develop into a real partnership."

"You know an impressive amount for a fifteen-year-old," Mrs. Whitely said.

"My mom taught me," Amy said. "Now that she's not here, Ty and I work together with the horses. It's been great experience."

As the words left her mouth, she realized what she was saying. Her breath caught in her throat. It was so natural to talk about working the horses together with Ty and for her to take their relationship for granted. And now it could be very close to coming to an end. Ty had hardly spoken a word to her since that morning, and whenever she had caught sight of him around the yard, his face had been serious and his eyes hard.

Just then, Claire came back. "OK," she said, snapping the lunge line on Flint. "Here goes."

She led Flint up to the training ring. "Remember, he can be a bit excitable at first," Amy warned, seeing the Thoroughbred's ears prick and his tail lift as he jogged up the path.

Claire nodded.

Amy opened the gate, and Flint pranced into the ring.

"Be careful, honey," Mrs. Whitely said.

Claire walked to the center of the ring. "Away!" she said to Flint.

With a joyful bolt, Flint plunged to the outside of the ring and bucked twice. Amy's heart stopped in her chest. *Stay confident, Claire,* she thought.

"And trot!" Claire said firmly, bringing the whip down on the sand behind him. "Trot on!"

Amy looked at her face. Claire's eyes were fixed on her horse. Her shoulders square to his, she urged him on. For a moment Flint hesitated and looked as if he was about to plunge again, but Claire brought the whip down on the ground again. "Flint — trot!"

With a toss of his head, the gray obeyed. Amy's hopes lifted as she watched.

"And canter!" Claire told the gelding firmly. Flint broke into a canter. Claire played out the lunge line and let him canter in large circles, and at last he started to relax and lower his head.

Amy felt like she could breathe normally again.

"Hey, she's doing really well," Mrs. Whitely said.

Claire slowed Flint and turned him before sending him off at a canter on the other rein. Her eyes were focused on the horse, and her face shone with a new confidence. After a bit, she halted him. "I'll take him off the lunge line now," she said.

"Are you sure that's a good idea?" Mrs. Whitely said.

Claire nodded. "He'll be fine, Mom."

Unsnapping the lunge line, she sent Flint to the outside of the ring. "And canter!" she said. Flint was just as responsive as the day before.

Watching Flint so willingly obey the commands and seeing the pride and delight on Claire's face, Amy felt a lump suddenly rise to her throat. She was so happy to see a horse and a human working together as equals, trusting and respecting each other. It was what Heartland was all about.

Hearing a noise behind her, she turned. Ty was standing a little way off. Suddenly, he saw Amy looking at him, and he walked away.

In the ring, Claire stopped Flint. "What do you think, Mom?" she said, leading him over, her eyes shining.

"It's amazing," Mrs. Whitely said in astonishment. "He did just exactly what you told him to."

"I know. He's so wonderful." Claire stopped Flint. "I *can* keep him, can't I, Mom?"

Mrs. Whitely smiled. "Yes, you can."

"Oh, thank you!" Claire cried. She threw her arms round Flint's neck. "Did you hear that, Flint? I can keep you!"

Flint nickered and nuzzled her arm as she hugged him.

Claire looked around in astonishment. "He's never done that before! He must be starting to like me."

"Well, now that we've decided you're keeping him, I guess we're going to have to start looking for a house with some land," Mrs. Whitely said to Claire.

Claire looked at her in surprise. "But we're already renting a house."

Mrs. Whitely smiled. "I was talking about a house to *buy*. I was thinking we could plan to stick around here for a while. My work's going well, and it seems like you're happy here." She paused. "And it would be nice for you to be close to your father. What do you think?"

"Oh, Mom, that would be fantastic!" Claire exclaimed. She turned to Amy. "Oh, Amy, isn't this great?"

Amy grinned. "You'll have to see Ashley every day!"

"Who cares?" Claire said. She kissed Flint's soft gray nose. "I've got Flint. Nothing else matters."

❧

Amy had just said good-bye to Mrs. Whitely and Claire when the phone started to ring. She ran to answer it.

"Hello, Heartland," she said. "Amy Fleming speaking."

"Hi," a woman's voice said. "Is it possible to speak to Ben Stillman, please?"

"You could, but he's out on a ride," Amy said. Suddenly, she caught sight of Red coming down the path. "Actually, he just got back. Who should I say is calling?"

"It's his mom."

Amy put the phone down and went to the door. "Ben! It's your mom!"

Ben dismounted and handed Red's reins to Amy. "Can you hold him for me?"

"Sure," Amy said.

She took hold of Red's reins, and Ben ran to the kitchen. Red was still breathing heavily from his ride. It looked like Ben had been riding him hard. Deciding she should start to cool him down, Amy started to walk him around.

Five minutes later, Ben came out of the house.

"What did your mom want?" Amy asked. Suddenly, she saw that his face was dark and angry. "Was it bad news?"

"She's not coming!" Ben said.

"Not coming?" Amy echoed.

"To the show."

"Oh, Ben, I'm sorry," Amy said.

Ben grabbed Red's reins. "I was stupid to believe that she really would. She always cancels at the last minute — always." His face hardened. "Well, from now on I'm just not going to care. She can do what she wants. It's just me and Red — that's all that matters." He put his foot in the stirrup and mounted.

"What are you doing?" Amy said in surprise.

"I'm going to practice for this show," Ben said. "Mom might not be there, but that doesn't matter. We'll show everyone just how good we are."

He clicked his tongue and Red walked forward.

"But, Ben, you just got back from a ride," Amy protested, walking beside him. "Red's still hot."

"That was just a trail ride," Ben said as he trotted Red toward the ring.

Hearing the clatter of hooves, Ty came out of the feed room. "What's Ben doing?" he demanded, coming across the yard. "I thought he jumped him hard yesterday."

"He did," Amy said. "And he took him out on the trails this morning. But he got a phone call from his mom, and then he went kind of crazy. He said he's going to take Red over some courses, but Red seemed awfully hot to me. He was really blowing."

"Well he shouldn't overdo it." Ty said grimly. "I think we should check it out."

He hurried across the yard. Amy followed him.

When they reached the training ring, Ben was cantering Red toward a jump. It was a three-and-a-half-foot spread that looked really high. All the fences in the ring were set higher than three feet.

"Ben! Stop!" Amy called, running up to the gate.

But Ben ignored her. He brought his whip down on Red's neck, and the chestnut just cleared the fence. Pulling him to a halt, Ben dismounted and raised the pole another foot.

"What are you doing, Ben?" Ty said, striding into the ring.

"Jumping my horse!" Ben said through gritted teeth. He swung himself onto Red's back. "Get out of my way!"

Ty didn't move. Pulling on Red's reins, Ben cantered the horse past him.

"Ben! No!" Amy said, her heart leaping into her mouth as she saw Ben turn Red into the jump. For one horrible moment she had a vision of her father jumping

Pegasus and the pole catching between Pegasus's legs, bringing the horse and rider crashing to the ground. Things had gone far enough! She couldn't handle Ben's being so careless — even if it was his own horse. She ran across the sand toward the jump. "Will you *stop*! Red's tired! It's too much for him! Let him have a rest."

But Ben wouldn't back down. He brought his stick down twice on the chestnut's neck. For one moment as Red approached the towering jump, it looked like he was going to take off, but then his courage failed him and he stopped abruptly, his hooves skidding in the sand.

"Come on!" Ben shouted, reaching back and hitting Red's quarters with the crop.

The horse panicked and bolted away from the jump, straight toward where Amy was standing. For a moment, all Amy saw was Red's frightened eyes and foaming mouth, and then she felt Ty grabbing her by her shoulders and pulling her out of the way.

"You idiot!" Ty howled at Ben, still gently holding Amy's shoulders.

Amy's heart felt like it would burst through her chest, it was hammering so hard. She caught the look of shock on Ben's face, and then his eyes darkened again. Turning Red toward the fence, he brought the whip down on Red's quarters.

"Stop it, Ben!" Amy screamed.

Seeing the jump, Red panicked and rose into the air. Taken by surprise, Ben threw himself forward onto Red's neck to stay on. Ty let go of Amy and ran across the sand, prepared to grab Red's reins as the chestnut landed.

Red shot backward in alarm but Ty hung on. "Steady, boy, steady!"

"What are you doing?" Ben shouted at Ty, recovering his seat and trying to yank the reins away from him. "Let go of my horse."

Ty held tight to the reins and gently patted Red's sweaty neck. The chestnut's chest was still heaving with deep breaths.

"I won't let go until you get off and let him cool down," Ty said. "Red's exhausted. You're working him too hard, too often, and he needs a break."

"Don't tell me how to deal with my horse," Ben said.

"It's your choice, but not while you're at Heartland." Ben glared at Ty.

"Just get off," Ty unexpectedly yelled. "Now!"

Ben let out a huff and pulled his leg over the saddle. He stared at Ty for a moment and then, turning swiftly, grabbed Red's reins and led him out of the ring.

Amy didn't know what to do. She looked at Ty's furious face and then at Ben disappearing across the yard. She stepped forward.

"Don't go after him, Amy," Ty said intensely.

Amy stopped and looked at him. "I have to. I just *have* to."

Ty's eyes bored into hers. "If you go, I'm leaving," he said. "I've had enough, Amy — I've *compromised* more in the last two weeks than in the rest of my life. I'm not prepared to stand by when I see cruelty like that, not even for you."

"What do you mean?" Amy whispered.

Just then there was the sound of shouting. Ben came running up to the gate. "Amy!" he yelled. "Amy! It's Red! Come quick!"

Chapter Ten

For a second, Amy glanced beseechingly at Ty and then ran to the gate.

"Red's collapsed in his stall!" Ben gasped.

Amy raced down the yard. When she got to Red's stall, she saw that the chestnut was violently trying to roll. "Colic!" she said, grabbing the halter from his door. "Quick! Get him up!"

Ben had taken Red's saddle and bridle off. Grabbing Red by his mane, he urged him to his feet. The chestnut scrambled up, but almost at once his legs began to buckle again. "Walk him around," she said, fastening the halter quickly. "You can't let him roll like that, or he could twist his intestines. I'll get Ty."

"Don't waste your time," Ben said. "Just call the vet!"

"I'll get Ty first," Amy said. She saw Ben's face drop.

"Ben — Ty is good at this stuff. He'll do whatever he can to help. This is more important."

She raced back across the yard. Ty was walking down from the training ring, his face set.

"Ty!" Amy gasped. "Red's got colic. It looks bad. Ben's walking him around." She grabbed his hand. "Please, Ty! You've got to come look at him. Please?"

Ty stared at her pleading expression. "You honestly think that I'd refuse to help because it's Ben's horse?"

"No, Ty — that's not it," Amy began to stammer.

Ty just shook his head and then strode across the yard toward Red's stall.

Ben was walking Red along the paddock. The horse's sides were damp with sweat and each step he took looked like a huge effort. When Ben saw Ty, his face tightened. But Ty ignored his expression. "Do you have any idea what could have caused it?" he demanded.

For a moment, Ben looked like he wasn't going to acknowledge Ty, but then his concern for his horse overcame him. "None. He was fine out on the trails," he said, stopping Red.

"Did he eat anything while he was out?" Ty asked.

"No. Well, nothing out of the ordinary. I stopped for a bit and let him graze on some grass at the side of a field."

"Mowed grass?" Ty said quickly.

"Of course not!" Ben said angrily. "And I didn't let him drink a troughful of water after it, either. I'm not stupid. I didn't purposely try to give him colic, you know."

"It's OK, Ben!" Amy said. "Ty's just trying to help."

Ben ran a hand through his hair. "Yeah, OK. I'm sorry. No, it wasn't cut grass." Just then Red's legs started to fold again. "Up, boy!" Ben cried, making him move forward.

"Amy, will you call Scott?" Ty said.

"Yeah."

Amy ran inside. But the receptionist at Scott's veterinary office told her that Scott was out on a call. "I'll get the message to him as soon as possible," she told Amy.

"Please hurry," Amy begged, looking out the window and seeing Red kick at the ground and try to reach around and bite at his flanks.

As she put the phone down, Lou came into the kitchen. "What's going on?" she asked, seeing Amy's worried face.

Amy quickly explained.

"That sounds bad," Lou said. "Is there anything I can do?"

Amy shook her head. "Not really, although you could call Scott's office back in ten minutes and see if they've gotten through and if they know how long he's going to be."

"Sure," Lou said. "And I'll get Grandpa."

Amy hurried outside and told Ben and Ty what was

happening. "They're trying to get in touch with Scott, but he's out on a call."

Grandpa and Lou came hurrying out of the house. Jack's eyes swept over the distressed horse. "It's colic, right?" he said to Ty.

Ty nodded. "But we don't know what caused it."

Suddenly, Red seemed to stagger. "He's getting worse!" Ben said.

"Keep him walking," Jack Bartlett instructed.

Ben moved Red on. "I can't believe it hit so quickly," he said. "Colic doesn't normally get bad so fast, does it?"

"Maybe it's not just colic," Ty said thoughtfully.

Ben turned on him. "Of course, it's colic! You can see the way he keeps trying to roll. What else could it be?"

"Do you have any ideas, Ty?" Jack said quickly.

"It could be some kind of poisoning," Ty said. "Colic might be just one of the symptoms."

"Poisoning!" Amy echoed, her heart dropping.

Ty was already hurrying over to Red. "Hold him still," he said to Ben. He opened the horse's mouth. "It could be poisoning, all right. Look at his gums — they're inflamed!" He turned to Ben. "What's he been eating?"

"Nothing, only grass!" Ben said desperately. "And I checked it out. There weren't any weeds or anything. It was just plain grass at the side of a field."

Amy's heart pounded. She knew that when treating

cases of poisoning you had to act quickly, but it was also vital to know exactly what type of poisoning it was so that the right remedy could be used, or there could be other side effects. How could they find out before it was too late what had poisoned Red?

"Where did you say the field was?" Ty demanded.

"I don't know," Ben said. "It was out to the south. It looked like it had just been seeded."

"Just been seeded?" Ty repeated.

"Do you think you know what the poison is, Ty?" Grandpa said.

Ty didn't answer. Instead he raised a hand quickly in front of Red's face. The chestnut shied back clumsily. Ty nodded. "That's it," he said grimly.

"What?" Amy demanded.

"Mercury poisoning," Ty said.

Ben stared at Ty. "But Red hasn't been anywhere near any mercury!"

"Organic mercury compounds are sometimes used as seed dressings," Ty said. "It's my bet that the field had been treated and some of the seeds drifted into the grass at the side."

Ben's face paled. "But mercury's really toxic."

Grandpa spoke quickly. "Is there anything we can do, Ty? Can we drench him? Give him something?"

"If it *is* mercury poisoning, then we have to get the mercury out of his system as fast as we can," Ty replied.

"If we don't, his kidneys will fail. We can try drenching him with a saturated sodium bicarbonate solution. That should help clear the mercury out."

"But what if it isn't mercury poisoning?" Amy whispered, looking at Red and then back at Ty. "What if the sodium bicarbonate doesn't help — or even makes things worse?"

"It's a risk," Ty admitted. "But there's no way to know exactly what it is right now. If we wait for Scott to get here, it might be too late." He looked at Ben. "It's your choice, Ben."

Ben hesitated. Red groaned and his knees buckled. "Treat him!" he said suddenly, as Red collapsed on the ground. "Do whatever you can!"

"Amy, Jack, can you help Ben get Red into his stall?" Ty said, starting to run across the yard. "It'll be better to work in a confined space. I'll make up the solution. Lou, can you call Scott's again and tell them that it's more than colic?"

Everyone did as Ty asked. Amy, Grandpa, and Ben forced Red to his feet. His legs were unsteady, but they managed to get him into his stall. Ben's face was pale as he turned Red in circles to stop him from lying down. "I don't know what I'll do if anything happens to you," he said, rubbing Red's face.

Ty appeared with three old plastic bottles filled with a saturated solution of sodium bicarbonate.

"It's OK. You can let him lie down," he said. "Just don't let him roll."

Ben let Red sink down onto the straw. Ty knelt down beside the horse's head and opened the first bottle. "Come on, boy," he said, tilting the horse's head back. "I know you're not going to like this, but I'm afraid we've got no choice."

Red struggled to get his head away as Ty began to tip the liquid down his throat. Ty slid his thumb in the side of Red's mouth to make sure the solution went down, but Red kept trying to pull away.

"Here, I'll hold him," Ben said, moving swiftly to Ty's side and steadying Red's head. With Ben there, Red calmed down.

"Don't hold his head too high, or he might choke," Ty said. "Angle it lower."

"Come on, boy," Amy whispered, kneeling beside him and stroking his hot neck. "You gotta do this to get better!" She glanced at Lou and Grandpa who were standing by the stall door watching tensely.

Ty finished one bottle and started on the other. "Are you sure this is right?" Ben said, looking at the stream of liquid being poured steadily down Red's throat.

"It's the fastest way to wash the poison out," Ty said. He finished the second bottle. "OK, let him rest a minute."

Ben let go of Red's head and, making a wisp from some straw, began to dry Red's sweating sides.

Amy saw the horse look uneasily around at his stomach.

"It's OK, boy," she said, moving up to his head and starting to work T-touch circles on his ears and face. "It's going to be just fine."

Amy's fingers worked skillfully. Horses that were ill often responded well to ear work. In a short while, Red stopped looking at his stomach and let his head hang low.

"He seems to like that," Ben said, coming and joining her. "Will you show me what to do?"

Amy explained how to do the circles, and Ben took her place at the Red's head.

Amy felt the chestnut's sides. His skin was still hot and damp, his flanks trembling slightly.

"His breathing's really shallow," she said in a low voice to Ty.

"Let's drench him again," Ty said, looking worried.

"I'll make some more solution," Grandpa said.

They kept up the routine for another half hour, alternately drenching and using T-touch circles.

"Come on, boy," Ben pleaded after they finished the third drenching. "You can make it!" He turned to Ty. "Isn't there anything else you can give him?"

Ty shook his head.

Ben buried his head in his hands. "He's got to get better."

"Keep working," Ty said grimly.

Just then, there was the sound of the phone ringing. "I'll get it!" Lou said, rushing toward the house.

A few minutes later, she came running back. "That was the vet's — Scott's on his way. They think he should be about twenty minutes." She looked at Ty in concern. "Will that be soon enough?"

"I hope so," Ty said.

Ben squared his shoulders. "It will be!" He started to work on Red's ears again. "It has to be."

Grandpa reappeared in the stall doorway and looked at the sodden, soiled bed. "He could do with some clean straw. Come on, Lou, give me a hand."

As Lou and Grandpa brought some clean straw and began to spread a thick layer over the bed, Amy felt Red's sides again. With relief, she realized that the skin under her fingers was not as steamy and no new patches of sweat were breaking out. "Hey!" she said. "I think he's calming down. In fact, I'm sure of it."

The others looked at Red. His head was still resting on the straw, but his eyes had lost the panic-stricken look of earlier, and his nostrils were no longer flaring with every breath.

"You're right!" Ben said. "Come on, boy!" he said dramatically. "You're going to make it."

Amy went to work with renewed vigor. *Oh, please,* she prayed, *please let this mean that Red is going to pull through.*

✥

Twenty minutes later there was the sound of car tires screeching to a halt outside the house.

"Scott!" Amy cried in relief as the vet appeared in the stall doorway.

"I came as fast as I could," Scott said, kneeling down next to Red.

"We think it's mercury poisoning," Ty said quickly. He explained about the grass that Red had eaten. "He was showing signs of nervousness and muscle weakness and had severe colic. We didn't know when you'd get here, so we took a chance and treated him. We've been drenching him with sodium bicarbonate solution."

Scott looked in Red's mouth and then stroked Red's neck. "You did the right thing. In fact, acting when you did probably saved his life." He looked at Ben. "He's your horse, right?"

Ben nodded. "Is he going to be OK?" he asked anxiously.

"I hope so. I'll inject him with some calcium disodium versenate," Scott said, checking Red's mouth again as he spoke. "It will offset any remaining mercury so it will pass through his system harmlessly. I'll take a sample of his stomach contents for analysis. But I think Ty made the right diagnosis. It looks like mercury poisoning to me." He stood up. "I'll get my things from the car."

"So he'll make a full recovery?" Jack Bartlett asked.

Scott nodded. "He'll need several more injections over the next couple of days, but I think he'll be back on his feet again soon."

As Scott hurried out of the stall, Amy sat back in the straw, feeling half dazed with relief. She pulled her legs to her chest and rested her head on her knees. Suddenly, all the tension that had been building up inside her over the course of the afternoon overwhelmed her. She gave a sob.

Ty and Ben looked around in surprise.

"Hey," Ty said, sitting down beside her and putting his arm around her shoulders. "You heard Scott. Red's going to be OK."

Amy nodded and sniffed. She felt so mixed-up and confused. She was delighted that Scott thought Red was going to be fine, but that didn't wipe away the events of the afternoon.

❧

When Scott had finished treating Red, he started to put his things back in his bag. "Looks like he's been through a war," he said, pointing to the whip marks still visible from earlier. "How did he get those?"

Amy glanced at Ben. His face was bright red. "Um — I —"

"Oh, that happened when he was turned out in the field," Ty said quickly. "He was just playing around with the other horses."

Amy saw Ben look at Ty in astonishment.

"Oh, right," Scott said, straightening up.

Grandpa had gone back to the house, but Lou still stood by the stall door. "Do you want to come in for a drink?" she asked Scott.

Scott smiled at her. "Sure," he said, picking up his bag. "That sounds good."

Lou opened the door for him, and they walked toward the house together.

Ben turned to Ty. "Thanks," he said quietly.

Ty shrugged.

"I mean it, Ty," Ben went on. "And not just for telling Scott that Red got those welts in the pasture. Thanks for everything — for realizing what was wrong with Red and for doing what you did. If it hadn't been for you, who knows what would have happened?" He crouched down in the straw and stroked the chestnut horse. "Red means more to me than anything," he said quietly. "He's all I have."

Ty looked questioningly at Ben.

Ben laughed bitterly at Ty's reaction. "Oh, I know you think I'm real lucky, that I've got it all, but it isn't as simple as that. My dad ran off when I was ten, and after that things fell apart. I started getting into trouble in school. My mom couldn't deal with me, so she sent me to live with my aunt." He looked Ty straight in the eye. "My aunt's been great, but she's always made it clear that she's got her own life to lead. I owe her a lot since she got me interested in horses and she gave me Red, but I never really knew if I belonged there. I felt like I was in the way. Then she told me that she wanted me to come and work here, and I resented it. All my life I've been shuffled around." He turned back to Red. "Anyway, I know I haven't handled things here well at all and that I'm not the only one who has stuff to deal with. It's just that I didn't want to be here in the beginning." He looked up at Amy and Ty. "I didn't want to have to start over again. I should have said something. I'm sorry to drop all this on you now."

"Actually, I — I knew about your parents getting divorced," Amy admitted. "Lisa told Lou." She felt Ty look at her.

"Did you all know?" Ben said, obviously embarrassed.

Amy shook her head. "Ty didn't."

Ben looked at Ty. "Well, now you do," he said. "And not that it's an excuse, but at least now you know. I'm not so good at dealing with people. Most of the time I feel like the only one who understands me or cares about me is Red."

"Ben," Amy reassured him, "that's just not true. Life isn't all black and white like that. There were reasons why your mom sent you to live with your aunt — I'm sure some were good and some were bad. Just like when Lisa sent you here. She probably did it because she hoped you'd get something out of it. She definitely cares about you. You have to know that."

"Maybe," Ben said. He smiled. "She got me Red, anyway." He gently touched the horse's face. "Training him was the first thing I was ever good at. My aunt bought him for me when he was three. No one else could ride him, but I did. And then when we started showing and we were winning, it was like something was finally going right."

Suddenly, Amy began to understand why Ben seemed so driven to win. He didn't just like it — he *needed* it.

Ben sighed. "I know we've had ups and downs since I got here, but I have enjoyed it — and I'll be sorry to go."

"Go?" Amy said in surprise.

"Yeah." He looked at her. "There's no way you're going to want me to stay after how I've been acting. And what I did to Red was wrong." He shook his head. "It was more than wrong. I was upset, and I took it out on him. There's no excuse for that."

"No, there isn't," Amy said honestly. "But if you're

really sorry, then we can try and work it out. But it's not just up to me. It's also up to Ty." She looked at Ty, who was staring intently at Ben.

Ben averted his gaze. "But I thought you'd hate me for what I did," he said to Amy. "I went against what Heartland stands for."

"I hate *what* you did," Amy said. "But I don't hate you." She looked at Red. "I know you care about Red, and you didn't mean to hurt him."

Ben nodded. "I'd never *mean* to hurt him, but I did. Now I have to try to regain his trust." He stroked Red's mane. "The worst part is, if he hadn't gotten sick from that grass, I wouldn't have thought twice about over-working him and forcing him to jump those fences. But seeing him so sick, I suddenly realized how much he meant to me and how right you were. I don't want Red to listen to me because he's scared, I want him to really want to work with me so we're a team." He met Ty's steady gaze. "If I can't stay, I'll understand. A lot has happened between us. But I want you to know I've learned a valuable lesson that I'll remember no matter where I am."

Amy looked at Ty, hoping he felt the same way she did.

He nodded. "It's OK, Ben," he said quietly. "You can stay."

Amy felt a rush of relief as she saw Ben's eyes light up.

"I'll work hard," he said quickly. "And I'll learn fast. I want to be a real part of Heartland."

Suddenly, Red nickered softly, half lifting his head from the straw.

"Hey, boy," Ben said softly, reaching out to stroke him. "You feeling better?"

Amy tried to swallow her tears as she saw Red lift his nose to Ben's hand and gently nuzzle his palm. Amy knew they had a strong bond, but she was sure that this would make the horse and rider even closer.

❧

Leaving Ben and Red in the stall, Amy and Ty went outside. "So how long have you known?" Ty said when they were out of earshot of the stall.

Amy knew what Ty was talking about. "For about two weeks," Amy admitted. "I couldn't tell you. Lou made me promise not to. She said it would be hard for Ben if he found out that we all knew. But it's been *so* hard keeping it from you. I know it wasn't fair. And I knew you'd be more understanding with Ben if I could tell you. It was so frustrating. I'm really sorry, Ty."

"Lou was probably right," Ty said. He ran a hand through his hair. "But it was really hard knowing that there was something you weren't telling me." He shook his head. "That's just not the way we are with each other.

At least now I know *why* you were sticking up for Ben — even if I still don't agree with it."

Looking at his tangled hair and the weariness in his eyes that reflected the stress of the afternoon, Amy realized there was something else she was keeping from Ty. "Oh, Ty," she said desperately. "Please don't leave. I need you here — we all do. Heartland wouldn't be the same. It would be nothing without you!"

"What are you talking about?" Ty asked, confused.

"I know you're thinking about going to Green Briar," Amy rushed on. "I'm sorry, but I heard you on the phone with Val Grant. I heard you say you'd think about it and let her know. But please, please don't go!"

There was a silence. "Amy," Ty said, his eyes searching hers. "Tell me honestly. Did you think, even for a second, that I wouldn't help Red because of what happened with Ben and me?"

Amy didn't hesitate. "No," she said desperately.

"Just like you know that I would never consider leaving Heartland to go to work at Green Briar," Ty said.

"But I heard —"

"You heard me say I'd let Val Grant know if I wanted to consider her offer." Ty said. "I told her I wasn't leaving Heartland, and she said to call her if I changed my mind. That's it," Ty said emphatically.

"But today," Amy replied, "today you said you'd leave if I went after Ben."

"Amy, if you had followed him, I would have been pretty mad and would have taken off. But I never would have left for good." Ty looked at Amy as his words started to sink in.

"So you're not going?" Amy said hesitantly.

"No," Ty said, shaking his head. "I'm not. I never even considered it."

"Oh, Ty!" Amy said, her eyes starting to shine with relief and delight. "I'm so glad! I feel bad that I thought you might go to Green Briar. I couldn't handle the idea of being at Heartland without you."

"Well, you don't have to." Ty took her hand and looked into her eyes. "My future's here at Heartland, Amy — with you." Ty said.

Amy smiled gratefully, relieved that things between her and Ty were back to the way they had been, knowing that they shared the same dream — the same future at Heartland.